S0-BAC-916

MISTER BRIDESMAID

IVY OLIVER

CHAPTER 1

JULIAN

The last day in paradise.

If you can call this paradise, anyway. At six-thirty in the afternoon, it's ninety degrees in the shade. Although I've been informed it's a dry heat, I don't feel dry at all. This whole trip I've felt like a fish out of water—at a fish fry.

My skin is dry, my hair is turned to straw, and I go into a sneezing fit every time I go from inside to outside, thanks to my sinuses. Every building roars a blast of cold air like an ice dragon when you walk inside, banishing the heat. This whole city is a monument to man's arrogance. Right now, the biggest thing on my mind is returning to Seattle and the nice, cool, humid world I've come to call home.

Well, second biggest thing on my mind. The biggest would be Colton Steele, my best friend's brother. At this very moment, he's a scant twenty feet away, cupping a neat whisky in one hand as if he's looking for the first opportunity to dive off the rooftop bar. Even scowling, he's so handsome it physically hurts to look at him, like a crushing fist in my chest. His dark hair is always tussled just so, self-organizing according to its own perfection. His eyes are a dark blue, the most striking aspect of his tanned, chiseled features. High cheekbones, strong nose, full lips.

I haven't seen him in six years and, in the interim, he hasn't really gotten older, only become more himself. He always filled out his clothes but now his massive shoulders and chest pull the striped fabric of a designer polo tight across his frame. When he breathes, I catch little glimpses of the outlines of ridged abdominal muscles on his belly and, if he moves just right, the untucked tail of his shirt reveals a sculpted V I'd like to trace with my tongue until he shoves my head between his legs.

Yeah. My BFF's older brother…reason why I know I'm gay. I messed around with Karen a little a long, long time ago, but I realized that despite our tweeny-bopper adolescent "dates" I had zero interest in her in that way, yet her brother brought me to full attention with just a word or a glance. Not that he often favored me with either. He disappeared from her life, pretty much, when the pair of us started high school. From then on, he became a ghost. Every once in a while, she'd show me a picture: Here he is parasailing. Here he is in ROTC. Here he is in his Navy whites. I filed all those away in the deepest vaults of my spank bank and never told my best friend, Karen, that I have a deep-seated thing for her brother.

"Thing" undersells it. Obsession. Infatuation. Hidden crush. Secret lust.

We've been in Las Vegas a week; he's been here the entire time, and I have yet to exchange more than six words with him. When he said hello to me, I was too shocked by his presence to offer more than a muttered "hi" and slip into hiding beneath his sister's metaphorical skirts. I hovered around the siblings during their tense catch-up sessions, like a potted plant someone forgot to water, before I slunk off to find something to do. Karen and Colton are not on the best of terms. That's a bit of an understatement: She goes full ice whenever he speaks to her and rarely starts a conversation.

That's the grind of this trip. Unless Karen has time to hang out, there's not much here for me to actually occupy myself with. A gambling mecca doesn't hold much interest if you've got no money to roll on the bones or whatever they say. So far, I've only managed to lose ten bucks in pennies to a one-armed bandit, and it totally satisfied my gambling-tooth. Why do people willingly play a game they call a bandit? That they know is going to lighten their wallets? What's the appeal?

So, I have nothing to do but try to wedge myself into hanging out with my best friend or fantasize about her brother bending me over a roulette table.

That mental image is going in the bank.

I'm here on Karen's dime. I'm in an odd spot: I'm serving as her Man of Honor in her wedding, which is apparently a thing now. The ceremony will be held tomorrow. On Key West. Yeah, she put up her extended family and friends in hotels in Vegas for a week before her wedding, we're spending another week in Florida after, and then she and her husband Alex are heading off to Europe for another two weeks after that.

Karen's parents are loaded. As is Colton, and as is Karen herself, though most of her fortune she got on her own. Though she doesn't act like it's anything special, Karen built a thriving online makeup business after moving a continent away from her parents. We all grew up on the East Coast—Karen is Mid-Atlantic Aristocracy and I'm the son of a waitress and a "traveling salesman" who only had a house because Mom inherited a half acre of what used to be a ten-acre farm.

I became fast friends with Karen starting in fifth grade and from there we were inseparable. You see, Colton attended private academies from pre-pre-school all the way to Harvard. Karen went to public schools with the likes of me.

Yeah.

Fast forward to my floundering freelancer career. Karen and her business are responsible for about half of the work I do.

My head is spinning in circles. Go talk to him. Go talk to him. Go talk to him.

I don't know why. It's a lost cause. He's straight as an arrow. Every once in a while, he'd text Karen a picture of himself with one or two stunningly attractive women in Dubai or Paris or wherever he was that week. I guess when he was in the Navy, he was an actual honest to God girl-in-every-port kind of guy, maybe two at a time. He radiates straightness like body heat off a panther. Yeah, I have no chance.

I mean, hell, he doesn't even look back at me when I stare right at him. What am I supposed to do, hike up my shorts and show some leg?

Karen bumps my arm with her fist and shakes me out of my weird session of mixed up fantasizing and internal complaining. She's wearing a giant straw hat and there's a smudge of sunscreen on her nose, just like every other day we've been here. The effort she's taken to avoid even a farmer's tan astonishes me, given she's arranged to be in the sun almost constantly for a month. She and Colton have the same coloring—inky dark hair, pale skin, blue eyes. Only he tans nicely and a hint of sun makes her explode in a profusion of freckles that cover her face and arms as densely as raindrops in a thunderstorm.

"Having fun yet?" she says.

We exchange looks and the answer is left painfully unspoken. I'm a fifth wheel here. Between her parents, relations, and distant friends, she's surrounded by people. We always used to lean on each other a lot; back when we first bonded, she and I were both awkward. I was skinny and gangly and she was plump and pimply. I grew skinnier and ganglier and she stretched out into a bombshell who can model her own products. If she were vainer, less driven, and her parents gave a shit, she'd be a runway model or a personality on television. I'm kind of glad they didn't. If they'd cared enough to prepare her for that kind of field, we'd never have met. I never tell her that, though.

The core of her personality never changed, though. She leans back against the railing and stands next to me, looking out over the Strip. We're on the rooftop of one of the big casino-hotels. Her parents insisted on booking the entire rooftop space every afternoon for the whole wedding party and the guests to mingle before breaking off for various activities.

So far, it's been all the usual stuff. Shows, casino runs, that kind of thing. She took a helicopter ride with her fiancé and some of her cousins of lesser wealth have been renting Ferraris and tearing around the desert. Tonight, though, is the bachelor/bachelorette party night and it's time to find out what I've been dreading to learn all day: Which side of the wedding party I'm going to be obligated to go with.

I have zero in common with her husband-to-be, and that's fine. I'm friends with her, not him, and I barely see the guy. It would be weird to join the bachelor party. I already told her I consider the whole thing kind of toxic.

"I want you to go with the guys," she says.

A sigh flows out of me like air from a deflating balloon.

"Oh, come on. What are you worried about?" she says, and then, "I want you to be my spy," softly.

I quirk an eyebrow. "Say what, now?"

"Lower your voice," she hisses, sharply. "I just want someone I trust to be there."

"Isn't your brother going?"

She doesn't go full on smirk, but her eyebrow twitches. "Yeah, he is."

Part of me wants to shout, I've changed my mind, I will gladly go, but I play coy.

Then it hits me. She wants someone she trusts. Her brother is still on the list of not-she-trusts.

"You really should talk to him," I shrug.

She rolls her shoulders and looks down at her feet.

"I've been talking to him. He can't hear me over the sound of what a perfect military hero douchebag he is."

They had a serious argument a few years ago. It was over the phone, but something made her just unload on him, start screaming. Before it turned hot, their conflict was a cold war. Things between them have been tense this entire time and he's just sort of floated along during all the activities, like a teenage boy at a middle school dance who's too cool to be there. It doesn't diminish his aloof debonair charm, but it is worrying.

"He met you halfway. He didn't have to be here."

There's a lot more to this argument than she lets on. I still don't know what the actual quarrel is.

"Are you worried about Alex?" I say very, very softly.

"Yeah," she says in a deadly whisper. "Well, not him. My cousin Trevor is here, and he's a douche."

I agree on the douche-ness of Trevor. When she says his name, I sneak a glance at him, over by the open bar pre-gaming. His hair and wraparound sunglasses make him look like someone put Guy Fieri on a diet and dumped a bucket of tanning chemicals over his head. Someone should tell him that pastel white board shorts and orange skin make him look like he works his day job in a magical candy factory.

My eyes slide right back to Colton, and Karen practically has to snap her fingers to get my attention.

"I figure if you're there, nobody will pressure the group into doing anything stupid, you know?"

"Yeah," I admit. "Yeah, that makes sense. So, less eyes-and-ears and more boat anchor?"

"That's not what I meant," she jabs back, her voice warbling back and forth between apologetic and annoyed.

"I should have just joined you in Florida. I don't fit in this crowd."

"Me either," she says, downing the last of her drink. "Having you around is the only thing keeping me sane. I try to hang out but someone is always trying to pull me away."

"Especially her," I say quietly, nodding to Bethany.

Bethany is one of Karen's many cousins, the kind of cousins who are constantly at each other's throats but must tolerate each other for social purposes. Karen and Beth belonged to the same sorority. Beth stalks, prowls, hovers. This is one of those family situations where Beth is from one of the "lesser branches" of the family, and she knows it. If the family tree was a river of money, she'd be on the fork of one of the tributaries. Nobody in the whole clan really has to work, but some are more equal than others.

Karen's dad is the firstborn son of a firstborn son and so on, so it all flows that way. There's some resentment there. Some scheming. Bethany has shark eyes, ready to roll over white when she sinks in her teeth.

Back then, Beth was like a lesser copy of Karen— shorter, squarer, with worse skin and limper hair. Karen rolled out of bed in the morning looking better and she quickly became the star of all their social circles, and Bethany hated it. When she showed up here, she'd been liposuctioned, bleached, and implanted. I overheard Colton remarking that she looks like a stripper. I've also noticed she's been showering Alex with attention all week.

Karen glances at me.

"I'm just nervous," she says. "It's something in the air. Look, you don't have to get wasted. I'd prefer that no one get wasted. We're flying out tomorrow at two and everyone has to be out of the hotel by eleven. I planned it that way."

I nod. "Yeah."

"You'll still have to peel Trevor out of a gutter by morning," she says, disgusted. "Look at him."

Trevor, presently, holds a superhuman quantity of beer in a long plastic container shaped like a trumpet with a giant curly straw. Disgusted, I clear my throat.

"We're going to break this up soon and my parents are taking the older family members to see Cirque. Meanwhile we celebrate our last night of 'freedom.'"

"I hate that," I say.

"So do I. Getting married shouldn't feel like going to prison. This whole destination thing was his idea, you know. I wanted to go to the Justice of the Peace and get this over with. Then my parents insisted on a ceremony and Alex jumped in with his huge plans. Aren't guys supposed to detest weddings?"

She's getting cold feet, or just nervous. Growing up,

Karen had crippling social anxiety, and it only started to fade when she grew into her genius, supermodel self, but it's still there. Despite her gorgeous looks and brilliance, she has to steel herself to do anything that makes her the center of attention. She must be pining for the chance to just be alone with Alex on their honeymoon.

My heart is starting to speed up. Going to a bachelor party with Colton. Whatever the party might entail, I might work up the courage to actually talk to him. I don't know why I want to. I'll just get hurt. It'll be like running face-first into a brick wall. With an erection. He hasn't even looked at me.

Except right now. His eyes snap down to his phone as I look over. Karen doesn't notice.

"Just do this for me, alright? I'm really going to appreciate it."

"Yeah. You know all you have to do is ask."

She punches my arm and taps her forehead against mine. It gets a few looks from distant members of the family and friends who might not realize I'm gay, or that we only do that because cats do it. We were those kinds of kids.

Yeah.

The pre-party starts breaking up. Alex's best friend Jeremy, also his Best Man, is the organizer and master of ceremonies, and he's started herding all the guys together. I drift over, halfway between invited and uninvited, in the awkward position of being sent by the bride.

Karen is over in the corner having a tense conversation with Colton about something I can't hear. In my secret realm of fantasies, I desperately hope she's trying to set us up.

She probably doesn't even know I like him.

Like? Listen to yourself, Julian. What am I, twelve?

Finally, he heads over, walking with a canted posture, shoulders bunched, like a bull who's picked out a plump runner who doesn't belong in Pamplona. He squares up next to me.

Jeremy and Trevor have hit it off, by the looks of things. Birds of a feather. They give Alex those challenging guy-pushes on the chest and shoulders as they loudly declaim the night's activities. We're going to a bar first, surprise surprise. I guess somebody rented a shuttle. That's good. I don't want to end up sloshed and stumbling around the streets of Las Vegas. I'm sure by the end of the night I'll have downed enough Cosmos to kill a bull elephant. I doubt I'm getting through this, either way.

So it begins. Jeremy and his co-conspirator Trevor make loud bullish calls and then everyone—about thirty guys—pile into two elevators, since one won't hold the entire group. I end up smashed into the corner—next to Colton.

God, what a sweet hell. It's just the outside of his arm pressed against my back, but the warmth is intoxicating, and I can smell him, earthy musk beneath leathery cologne. He sniffs the air—though he isn't the only one—as if to ask who's wearing the flowery scent. That'd be me.

The doors open and the press ends. I gravitate towards him, hoping that maybe sometime this decade I'll work up the courage to say something like "hi" or "so, how do you feel about this objectifying ritual of toxic masculinity?" but before I even formulate any words, I'm swept along with the crowd through an opulent palace of a casino lobby and out into the blasting heat and sunlight and again into the dark, in the back of a shuttle van. The shuttles are big, hulking cargo vans with lifted roofs painted black with graphics.

They, uh, also have stripper poles.

Yeah.

Then again, it's Vegas. The airport had stripper poles squirreled away somewhere.

Tucked in between two guys I don't know, I fiddle on my phone during the interminable ride down the Strip. Day or night, the traffic is obscene, with solid walls of cars crawling from stoplight to stoplight at five miles an hour, waiting what seems like hours for endless tides of cargo shorts and Hawaiian shirts to flow from sidewalk to sidewalk.

Finally, they dump us at a bar. The bright baking sun and brilliant blue sky, with not a single cloud, make it incongruous to be piling inside, but, as they say, it's five o'clock somewhere—and anyway, it's seven o'clock here.

It doesn't hit me just what type of bar it turns out to be until we're inside. Rhythms pulse, party lights dance, and every surface is either mirrored or chromed, even the bouncer's sunglasses. Everything is centered on the main attraction: Half-naked women gyrating on aluminum posts.

Yeah. I'm a fish out of water and the water is wearing a thong.

I get pulled along, realizing I need to stay close or they might literally forget me; I'm pretty sure neither Jeremy nor Trevor give a shit that I'm here, if they even counted me. Getting stranded in a strip club to miss my flight to my friend's wedding is pretty low on my bucket list.

So, I keep an eye on the guys and head for the bar. A little liquid courage will get me through this.

The bartender does an admirable job of scrunching her cleavage. I'm half-tempted to tell her she's wasting her time but end up leaving as generous a tip as I can muster anyway. Call it an A for effort.

"You're with the party?"

"Yeah," I say.

"Drinks are on the party tab," she says, appreciatively tucking the crumpled dollar bills into the tip jar.

That's what I needed to hear. I throw back a swig of Corona and turn only to nearly jump out of my skin. Colton has appeared at the bar beside me.

"Scotch whiskey, neat. Whatever you call top shelf."

"Sir, that's eighty dollars a shot," the bartender protests.

"So, pour it carefully," he says, smooth as silk.

Meanwhile I stand there gaping, and nearly drop my beer.

"Do I have something on my shirt?" he says, side-eyeing me. "You've been staring at me since we got here."

"Oh, sorry," I say, looking away. "I'm not really interested in this kind of thing."

"I mean here as in the city, not here as in this dive. You're Karen's best friend, right? I remember you from when you were fourteen."

Oh my God, if you are listening just strike me dead right here. Please just don't make it hurt, okay?

Colton snorts as he takes his drink.

"Yeah. I remember you, too," I say, trying to be sly. I think my voice cracked a little.

"Weird to see little Karen getting married," he shakes his head. "It's like I stepped away and everyone got old while I was gone."

"I'm old?" I chirp, lamely.

He snorts. "No. I am."

"You don't look old. You look pretty much like you did when you left."

"Flattering, but no," he says, touching his side. I glance at his impossibly taut stomach in profile and wonder what he was indicating. Whatever it was, his shirt covers it.

"I never pegged you for the strip club type," he says.

"You last saw me when I was in my teens. This is the longest conversation I've had with you in my life."

He snorts. "You can tell. Trust me, look at that jackass," he points at Trevor, who has three strippers giving him a lap dance at once, "I bet when he was fourteen, every other word out of his mouth was *titties*."

The bartender gives Colton a reverent look as she pours him a second drink. I barely noticed him draining the first.

"So, what are you doing here?" he says.

"You want the truth?"

"Yeah," he says. "I'm big on truth."

"No telling anyone," I say. "Cross your heart."

He makes the little gesture and my own heart nearly skips. I swallow hard.

"I'm a spy. Karen planted me in the crowd to keep an eye on things."

Colton laughs, a sound like velvet being drawn over steel. He eyes me and eyes his drink.

"Funny. I'm here for the same reason."

"She talked you into it?"

"No," he says, a quick shake of his head. "She told me not to cause trouble. She's afraid I'll make a scene with her boyfriend." He draws out the word, punctuating both syllables, "boy-friend," as if to highlight that he didn't title the guy her fiancé.

"So, why are you here?"

"Same as you," he says, offering his drink at me. I stare at it for a second and realize it's a toast.

I tap my bottle against the rim of his glass and murmur Karen's name. For a heart-squeezing second, I think our hands might actually touch. Get a grip, Julian.

"So, you're spying."

"Keeping an eye on, more like. I get a bad vibe from this guy's friends. They seem like the type to get him hammered and top off this evening with him in the champagne room with a blowjob."

"There's no sex in the champagne room," the bartender mutters.

"Sure there isn't," Colton says, smiling at her. He waves his glass.

"Maybe you should slow down," I say.

"Maybe you should sack up and have a real drink," Colton laughs. "Give him one too."

She pours me the same stuff she offered him and slides the glass my way. I reach for my wallet for the tip and Colton waves me off, smoothly slipping her a folded hundred-dollar bill. She nods appreciatively and steps aside to serve another member of the party.

"So," he says, nodding at the tumbler on the bar in front of me. "Drink."

Hesitantly, I lift the glass and sip some. It tastes like giving an exhaust pipe a blowjob. I almost drop the class, coughing, and wash out my mouth with citrusy pale beer.

"Don't have a lot of practice, I see," he says.

"I have plenty of tolerance. I just enjoy drinks that actually taste good. I don't see why everything has to be a contest to see how much dick swagger you roll, you know?"

He laughs. "Yeah."

I glance over at the stage. "How long do you think I'll have to sit here?"

"Couple hours," he says, shrugging.

"That long?" I sigh. "They're just tits. You can't tell me none of these guys has seen tits before. What's the appeal?"

He quirks an eyebrow with me. Despite being the manliest manly man that ever manlied he looks remarkably like his sister when he does that, and it gives me a little chill.

"That's an odd question."

"I'm gay," I shrug.

Maybe it's the booze, not that I've had much to rely on that for an excuse. The impulse has me blurt it out before I can manage to contain myself and then, like an idiot, I'm staring longingly into his eyes hoping for any kind of a signal that he might be interested.

He looks away before I can complete my search. Damn it.

Well, he didn't run off screaming. In fact, he's still standing there. Only a foot away, but he might as well be on the other side of the planet. A flash of light catches my attention. The rest of the guys are crowded around a stage show. When I look back, Colton is looking right at me.

I finish my drink. The taste is horrible and it makes me shiver all over. Colton leans casually against the bar and motions for another drink. His third.

"Maybe you should slow down," I say.

"Pretty much the only way I can stand this," he says in a low, husky voice.

"I thought you were a party animal," I say.

He does that eyebrow-quirk again.

"How would you know that?"

"Karen shows me pictures," I say, sheepishly. I neglect to add that I memorize them and masturbate to them, picturing him fucking me.

"Does she, now," he says. "I hadn't sent her any."

"I guess she stalks you on Facebook," I shrug.

He glances at me. "So that's what you think of me. Party animal?"

Before I can answer, there's a call over the loudspeakers inviting our entire party up to the upstairs lounge. A pair of strippers flanks Alex and leads him up the staircase. In place of the tassels of the old burlesque dancers, their bras bear sparklers on the pointed cups, lighting up the dark room around him.

With a bone-weary sigh, I fall in line. Colton is behind me. I can smell him, his unique mix of scents rising above the chaotic mess of the club. The world around me is ashes, stale beer, and just a hint of either old vomit or cheap melted chocolate bars. Somehow Colton's scent floats to the top, an overpowering blend of his deliciously manly natural scent and that leathery deodorant he wears. I think his chest just bumped into my back.

When we arrive on the second floor, it's time for everyone to crowd into a bunch of booths. This is a big place. I barely realized how big. There's a second level looking down on the main stage and a bunch of poles up here.

I start looking for a seat when a strong hand grabs my arm.

Colton.

Oh my God he's touching me. I almost let out a little squee noise. God, what am I, fourteen? I'm a grown-ass man. My hesitation ends after a second tug and I crush in beside him, between him and the end of the booth.

The drink of the night is vodka. Trevor and Jordan got us bottle service, meaning cocktail waitresses are strutting around in thigh-high boots pouring top-shelf stuff from magnum-sized bottles. The display is as much the focus as the drink; they each bend artfully at the hip, poking their asses straight out. Their costumes are so skimpy, the only way to tell they're waitresses and not strippers is that their clothes aren't designed to come off easily.

Sigh. Yawn. Seriously. I slump against the side of the

booth and wait my turn. Glasses are raised, Trevor yells something in brospeak, and the drinking begins.

Vodka goes down easier, but I'm no fan of drinking hard liquor straight. Next to me, Colton grimaces. He leans slightly to his side and speaks to me, and my heart flutters. He remembered I exist.

"I hate vodka," he mutters. "Doesn't taste like anything and top shelf shit is the same as comes in a plastic bottle for five bucks. Clear liquor is clear liquor."

"I could go for an appletini or something," I mutter.

Colton laughs, but there's no scorn in it. He snaps his fingers and the bottle service girl comes over, offering more, but he waves it away.

"Go fetch us two appletinis," he says.

She looks at him like he just asked her to take a swan dive onto the downstairs stage but rushes off to get what he asked. When she returns, he gives her a healthy tip, takes both drinks, and hands me mine.

"There you go," he says.

He takes a drink of his and looks at it, cocking his head to the side like a wolf who just heard an unusual noise.

"Huh. Not bad."

I laugh now and start nursing my drink. I'm already pretty tipsy and I don't want to get any drunker. If I space things out, I'm sure I can keep myself to that perfect level of tolerance for this bullshit I need to keep up with for the evening.

Then Jordan, he of groom-brothery and party-plannery, points us out.

"What the fuck are you two drinking?" he shouts.

Colton's expression darkens, and I have a sense—almost a vision—of him dumping his drink on the floor and taking his fists to the groom's brother, which would probably be a bad idea. By the time I grab his wrist, it seems like the storm has passed.

Trevor spots my hand and it's like a private, unspoken joke ripples through the group. He snaps his fingers, but not for more booze. Rather, he calls over a stripper, tucks a hundred-dollar bill into her G-string, and sends her my way.

I resign myself to sitting back and thinking of England. Not that I mind looking, you see, it's just that...meh. I can tell she's hot, I just don't have any interest in her.

Even when she mashes her giant boobs in my face. I thought there was a rule against touching the girls. I guess they can touch you. I actually yelp when her nipple pokes my eye. Yeah.

All of this is a source of great amusement to everyone present at this party. They've made me the butt of a joke. Great. I know Karen meant well. It would be some points for Alex if he put a stop to this and directed his bachelor party to, you know, party, not humiliate me.

"That's enough," Colton grunts.

I didn't get her name. She looks up and grins at him.

"You want a turn?"

"No. He's done."

"It hasn't been three songs—"

He shoves a folded sheaf of bills at her and shoos her with a motion of his hand.

I sink back into my seat, trying to disappear into the aged vinyl. Colton straightens himself next to me and looks down with almost tender concern that makes my heart do a backflip and face plant into my spine.

"You alright?"

I nod, vigorously. "Yeah. Fine."

"Want another one?" he says, hefting his appletini.

"I'm good for now."

I can see him debating whether to order another one for himself; his jaw works, like there's a thick piece of leather clenched in his teeth. With a shrug, he switches from gulping to nursing.

My buzz is coming along pretty good. I'm jovial when I drink, ready to joke around, and by the time the rest of the party is distracted by more strippers, I'm prepared to laugh the whole thing off.

Colton appears deeply offending, brooding into his appletini. It takes supreme brooding skills to pull off brooding into blue liquor.

Remembering why I'm here, I keep an eye on Alex. I doubt Karen had any idea where we were headed. The girls might be at one of the many "nude male revues" (for some reason if there's dicks it can't be a strip club) in town, so I can't judge, and Alex is being a gentleman. He even waves off a lap dance, basically dumping the girl on Trevor's lap, which takes his attention off me. I relax a little and check my watch.

Shit, it's not even eight o'clock. This is going to take hours. Resigning myself, I order appletini numero-two-o and accept that I need more social lubricant to slip through this night unscathed.

Colton

"Look," Karen said to me, "Just keep an eye on him, okay? He thinks I'm sending him to spy but Bethany will pitch a bitch if I bring him along on my bachelorette party. She's been nagging me to leave him behind all week."

"If he doesn't want to go, why not just let him stay back?" I said back.

My sister has more of my mother in her than either of them would care to admit. When she plants her fists on her hips, cants her head forward, and digs in her heels, she can be more intimidating than my father. I knew I wasn't going to move her, so I accepted guard duty. Keep watch over her best friend.

Now I just feel old and tired. I've got six or eight, even ten years on most of the guys here and this kind of adolescent bullshit is so far behind me I can barely see it. In a way, I feel like a chaperone for the whole group. Not just a chaperone for the chaperone.

It doesn't help that I feel strange every time I look at her friend. Julian. I remember him as a gawky, awkward teenager clinging to my sister's side. I, and I think everyone else, presumed it was puppy love. If I didn't know better, I'd figure him for a jealous hanger-on, here to wallow in self-pity as his dream girl gets married to another guy. Hell, that might be why the rest of the group is mocking him—they got the same impression.

I knew he was gay before I got here. I talk to Karen a few times a year. We're not close, but we don't hate each other. It's more of an unspoken tension. She resents me, and, in a way, I resent her. We both know that. My parents treated us very differently growing up—both doted on me, the future head of the family. There are expectations. Karen was free of those, but being free of your parent's dreams is a double-edged sword. She just sort of exists in the family, and Mom talks about her makeup company—the most successful business venture a family member has started in a generation—with mild disinterest or a kind of aristocratic disdain for her girl child getting her hands dirty with actual work, something best left to the province of men.

Neither of our parents have worked a day in their lives. They both inherited fortunes and Dad occupies his time with studiously pretending he manages the firm that bears our name. Curiously, though, nobody seems to have any concern about him going missing for a month for his daughter's ludicrous destination wedding.

A wedding which has been my bane for the last six months, since they announced. Mom has turned the joy of her daughter's nuptials into a bludgeon against her lothario son. "When," she keeps asking, "will I get married?" It's almost embarrassing that little Karen is getting hitched before the scion of the family.

Like those two are an advertisement for marriage. If wedlock looks like my parents' life, then to hell with it. I'll keep my freedom.

He keeps looking at me.

I'm not one of those guys who gets offended by a gay guy paying attention. Hell, it's a compliment, it's like being checked out by a woman. I'm a stud, so what. I blow it off. There was a lot of that when I was in the military—I served during Don't Ask, Don't Tell, which translated into a lot of sidelong glances and people feeling each other out before anyone brought anything up.

What confuses me about this is that my eyes keep wandering to him. I've been…curious, before, but not this curious. He's got everything that draws my attention to another man. He's tall and slim with a runner's physique, more muscle in his legs than his upper body, and a wild mop of hipster hair. He has that avocado toast and macchiato look, but beneath that is a femininely boyish face with full lips, big eyes, and soft skin. Something about him makes me want to protect him.

He wouldn't be the first one. I've been close to guys like that before, but I never acted on these urges. Even after a dozen whiskeys or…appletinis.

So, when I pull the stripper off him, my motives are purely altruistic. I give her a big tip, and my brain is thankfully not sloshing around in enough booze just yet for me to make a quip about complimenting her surgeon on his good work with her enhancements. I am not that crass, so at least I have that going for me.

Julian relaxes into his seat and knocks back more of this weird tasting booze he likes. It's not bad, but I'm pretty sure these would be headache city. Better than vodka, at least. To me, the top shelf stuff just tastes like aluminum. Bottom shelf like cheaper aluminum.

My gaze keeps wandering back to him. To his hands, his chest, his stomach when he breathes, the way the toes of his hiking boots cut little circles in the air. The booming beat of the club music jars my spine and catches my heart-beat, speeding it up in time with itself as my eyes rake him.

Then when he looks my way I yank my eyes in the other direction, like a flirty teenager who doesn't know how to sack up and make a move. I've felt this urge before, but it's never been this strong. A dumb notion wiggles its way through my mind and I have to bite down on it to keep the laugh from escaping my lips—I wonder what that insecure douche brother of the groom and Karen's cousin would say if I grabbed Julian and rammed my tongue down his throat.

Either they'd sit there and take it or I'd kick all their asses. These little boys wouldn't last five seconds with me.

Julian taps my arm.

"You okay?" he says, his words a little slurred and slow.

"Just fine," I say, raising my empty glass. "More!" I bark.

The waitresses here are good. There's another one coming before the empty glass is out of sight. They give one to Julian, too. Taking his cue, I slow down. If I have a drink in my hand at all times, it'll appear more like I'm enjoying myself and not choking down every passing second waiting for this embarrassing night of unimpressive hijinks with tedious people is finally over. I'm sure after all this that idiot Trevor will have himself puffed up like he's Hunter S. Thompson and this is *Fear and Loathing in Las Vegas*.

Give me a break.

My desperation to get out of here rises with each lap dance I wave off. I sense the moment is near when the guys drunkenly get up and lurch to the balcony to watch the floor show. The club is packed now, the music has ramped up, and I stand behind Julian, as bored as he is as the stars of the evening's entertainment rush out onto the stage. Posters on the way in said some porn star I've never heard of will be in the house tonight.

Standing behind Julian, something begins to happen. My eyes settle on the back of his neck. He has that kind of pale skin that never tans, just burns, and he's been hiding inside as much as he can manage. Pale skin peeks out above his collar. Tracing down the narrow, athletic lines of his back, my eyes fix on his ass. A perfect round bubble butt that turns me on more than any bethonged derriere in the house.

So that's how it starts. Blood starts to pump downwards, filling in between my legs. The tension rises with my dick, stiffening in my dark jeans. I'm glad I didn't wear something less restrictive. With no one looking, I can shift easily and hide my—

Julian takes a step back and bumps right into my dick. A shock, like someone touched an electrified prod to my skin, ripples from between my legs through my whole body. He looks over his shoulder and my mind conjures an image of him doing the same—slack, anxious expression and all —as my cock disappears into his ass, gliding between pale cheeks as ecstasy floods my body and he quivers all over, overwhelmed by my size and girth, a little moan escaping his lips as—

Fuck me, get a grip, Colt.

Julian's eyes snap away and he looks down at the stage as if he actually cares about the half-naked gyrations taking place below us. His shoulders are quivering. Hell, his whole body is quivering. Is a similar image running through his mind? Is he wondering what it'd feel like to take me inside him? It's good my hands are occupied. They want to loop around him and skim down his stomach and between his legs so I can grab his cock. I've always wondered what it would feel like to have one in my hand. In my mouth. Take control of him. Eat him all up.

Christ, he's Karen's best friend and I'm old enough to be his...actually, not old enough to be his anything, we're only six years apart, but it feels like decades. Twenty-four to thirty is still a big gap, especially after you've seen everything I have.

I've gone from hoping I can get through this night without vomiting on the groom to hoping I can get through this night without groping the bride's best friend. My sister's best friend. Very nice, Colton.

Can we leave now?

I motion for another drink. If I don't have to drive, I might as well take advantage of it. Maybe if I down enough I'll get struck by whiskey dick. Tonight, I may be the only man in the history of erections who's tried to go limp. It's not working. I can't get that image out of my mind.

What would it feel like?

I'll never know. I don't dare find out. I certainly don't dare smell his hair as we pile into the van.

Oh, damn it. He smells a little perfumey, but it's not heavy or overpowering. Could even just be flowering deodorant. He didn't notice, and I don't think anyone else did either. I crowd in next to him, squeezing him into the window, shielding him from the rest of them. I'm starting to act protective. Possessive. It's going to get me into trouble. When has it ever not?

"Where are we going now," Julian grumbles, talking more to himself than to me.

"Something else stupid," I muse, and it draws a giggle out of him. "I wonder if Mom and Dad knew where we were headed when they went off to Cirque du Soleil."

"Probably," Julian mutters. "They were young once, too, right?"

"Have you met them?"

Keep your mouth shut, Colton. You're boozed up, don't know what you might say. Julian laughs oddly, in a slightly forced way, and gives me a curious look. Has he heard stories? I'm sure he's heard all about my parents from Karen; she's never been shy of complaining about them to me, of course.

"Yeah," he says. "Only for about five minutes, though. Karen wanted to keep me away from them, I think."

I wince. I know Dad's stance on…I don't even want to think about the word he uses for gay men. Let's just call him traditional and leave it at that. I need another drink.

"He probably figured we're in a club-club."

"Like dancing?"

"Like leather chairs, cigars, and geopolitics," I say.

He dragged me to a few places like that before I started my naval career, to meet Important Men who talk about things they have no control over, feeling significant as they slug cognac and pretend to know anything about economics or social policy. I didn't mind the cognac, but the conversation was interminable, and *old*. I think they fancied themselves some kind of explorer's club from the nineteenth century but they just looked absurd trying to pull it off.

Surely, they'd never think of their kids partaking in the sleaze that permeates this city. It's just good old family fun. They have a way of seeing only what they want to see.

Suddenly I'm maudlin. At least it killed my unwanted hard-on for my sister's BFF. I have to remind myself, if he was a woman, I wouldn't go for it either. It would be considered rude, and a little predatory.

Predatory. Julian reminds me of some kind of exotic cat, both predator and prey animal, every movement languid and seductive in a casual, unknowing way, his sardonic smile unaware of how he captures my fantasies.

Ugh, another week of this and I can go back to my life.

Looks like the next stop on our journey is a casino crawl. The shuttle stops on the Strip and it begins—a slow-rolling tide of bros in popped collars flowing from casino floor to casino floor, starting with the Luxor near the airport, the one with the big pyramid.

I follow them inside. Julian is clearly nervous. It's Trevor, the little weasel, that notices first. He crowds the whole group around a craps table, edging in around an old man in a fishing hat who leans over the rail and ignores the world around him as he mechanically places bets and watches the dice roll. He doesn't even react when the leaders of this drunken excursion proclaim the occasion and barrage Alex with back-slaps and applause from the dealers.

Julian edges into the end of the table and doesn't even bother pulling out his wallet. It hits me that he probably doesn't have enough to play. It doesn't matter, there's so much activity that he can just watch, probably as bored as I am. I don't bother with any chips, either.

The dice work their way around. The table is having

rotten luck but to hear the cheering from this group, you'd think every roll is a seven-come-eleven. The croupier offers Julian the dice, and when he waves them away, the whole crowd jeers him. The wall of boos hits like a wave and the fine hairs at the base of my neck rise as my back tenses. Fuckers are getting off on embarrassing him. Trevor and Jordan lead the catcalls, but Alex has joined in too, the prick.

I throw down a sheaf of hundreds in front of Julian and direct the dealer to slide the chips to him.

"I'll stake you," I say. "Don't lose too much."

"I have no idea how this game works," he says, his voice almost pleading, nearly drowned by the cheering.

"Just do as I say and roll the dice when I tell you too," I murmur in his ear.

He goes erect—I mean, he stands up straight—and nods. I tell him where to put his first bet. Mollified, the stickman taps the table, indicating for him to throw. He grabs the dice and tosses them.

Briefly: Setting the many side bets aside for now, the game of craps is simple. Roll the dice. If they come up seven or eleven, you win your side bet. If you roll any number but two, three, or twelve, the objective then becomes to roll that number again, without rolling a seven first.

Julian's first roll is a seven. Winners all around, except for the sour old man in the fishing hat who bet the wrong way, meaning he placed a bet for Julian to roll a craps number.

His *second* is a seven, too. The pit boss—the guy who sits in the middle of the table—side-eyes him, but it's for show, not his money. Julian's third roll is a six- four and two.

I lean over and whisper—shout—in his ear.

"You have to roll a six again before a seven. Listen. Grab four green chips," I don't tell him that's $200, "toss it to the stickman, and yell 'hard six.'"

He does as ordered.

For the first time tonight, I smile.

After all the bets are down, the stickman sends the dice back. Julian picks them up and throws them. I lean over his shoulder, watching. For one pulse-pounding second, I think he did it—one of the dice turns over with three pips, but the other, five. An eight. I breathe a sigh of relief. If it'd come up four, making for seven, he'd lose all the money he bet.

The dice come back. He throws them.

Eleven. Cheers as the one-roll betters collect their winnings; betting eleven pays fifteen-to-one odds.

He rolls another eleven, and the cheers get louder. Craps has its own esoteric language; somebody yells, "Hey yo, back to back." "Yo" is the name for eleven.

Another roll. Twelve this time. A few Come betters—there's a spot on the table called the "Come Line," and, of course, the "Don't Come Line," and it gets complicated—grumble at their loss.

Again. Three.

Again. Five.

Again. Eight.

My nerves begin creeping up. The more he rolls, the more chances he has to roll a seven and lose, seven being the easiest number to roll. Six and eight are the second easiest, though, with equal chances.

Julian, shaking, must realize this, too. There's a building tension around the table.

His next roll bounces right out of the table.

"Say same dice," I bark in his ear.

He jumps and bumps into my side and repeats the

command. After another member of the bachelor party finds it on the floor, the dealers inspect the die and they come back to him.

My eyes linger on his delicate features. His prominent Adam's apple bobs as he swallows. He glances at me, feeling the pressure. There's a small fortune on the table and it's all riding on his next roll.

Swaying a little, he picks up the dice and tosses them, just hard enough to bounce against the far end of the table and roll back.

God damn it, the one die turns over on three pips. The other fucking stands up on its corner and spins in a circle before it falls. For a heart-clenching moment I expect that four to come up.

It's another three pips. Hard six. Winner.

The stickman taps his pole in front of Julian and announces his winnings, to be paid by the dealer next to him.

"Eighteen hundred," he says.

Julian almost collapses as he picks up over two thousand dollars off the table from his hard six and the winnings and odds on his line bet. It's still his turn until he "sevens" out.

His next roll isn't as fortuitous as the first. He rolls a five, then an eight, then a seven, to disappointed sighs.

"Hand the dealer all your chips and say, 'Color.'"

He blinks. "What? Why?"

"They'll change your chips for bigger denominations and we can go cash them in."

After his winnings have been color checked, I count out what I originally gave him and hand him back the rest.

He holds the chips, confused. "Aren't these yours?"

"You rolled," I say. "Cashier's over here."

Away from the table, the inside of the casino is cooler.

Julian sways on his feet as we wait for the cage. I don't know if it's from booze or the heady rush of winning at a game of chance. Once he's changed the chips, he stares at the cash like it's not real before he hastily stuffs it in his wallet. I, more casually, tuck mine back into my money clip.

"Bleh," he mutters, heading for the table.

I grab his arm and flinch. The booze and the casino atmosphere are getting to me. I shouldn't have touched him like that.

He turns around and looks at me.

"Let's have a seat for a minute, huh?"

"Yeah," he says.

I guide him to an empty roulette table and we take a pair of chairs, watching the bachelor party piss away their gambling budgets in a storm of cheers and calls for booze. Watching the casino employees and judging their reactions leaves me pretty sure that the party is cheering everything, even if they're losing. Someone yells "winner winner chicken dinner" and everyone who's paid to be there rolls their eyes in annoyance.

That phrase is probably drilled into their fucking skulls by now.

Julian yawns and clutches his head.

"You alright?"

"Fine," he mutters. "Little bit of a headache."

"If you'd drink real man's liquor you might not have that problem. I'd hate to be you in the morning."

He gives me a weary look. I flag a passing cocktail waitress. She has a small supply of bottled water, little half-pints, and hands him one. He drinks it like a thirsty man who's just crawled from hot sands onto the soft grasses of an oasis and sits back.

"I've already gotten a cotton mouth," he mumbles.

My gaze travels to his lips, caressing them with phantom fingers. Soft lips. The haze of stubble on his chin only makes him more intriguing, somehow. Leaning back, I almost rest an arm on his chair. My hand wants to sink into his hair, feel silky softness curling about my fingers. He stretches, arms back over his head, and I wonder how his skin tastes. Is there hair on his chest? Is it shaved? Naturally smooth?

Then comes the heady, disoriented feeling I get whenever I look too closely at another man, thinking about his body. His dick. He's got more of a bulge than I thought at first, or maybe he's at half-mast, too.

The two of us sit in silence and watch the idiots cheer and jump up and down over losing their money. Fishing Hat Man glances from side to side as if he's questioning his life choices but keeps playing with the smirk of a man who's betting the wrong way and the craps keep coming. Judging by his stack of chips, the others are losing money hand over fist.

Eventually they get tired of it. Craps is the only game that accommodates a big crowd. Some of them head off to the blackjack tables, others to roulette. I lead Julian around and explain the games to him.

This is Vegas. Most casinos elsewhere no longer play baccarat, but they have it here. I start humming the James Bond theme and lead Julian to the table.

"What's this?"

I explain the rules of Baccarat—which basically amount to a coin toss against the house but using a point system on cards instead of a coin. When you really think hard about the game, it's kind of dumb. The older version from when Ian Fleming was writing his secret agent stories involved some actual skill, like a poker game against the house, but it's changed since then. The odds were too good. It's still the best game in the house.

I sit down, cash in, and Julian stands behind me, leaning on my chair. Leaning over my head to watch, he rises on his toes and crosses his legs while standing. Glancing over my shoulder, I wish I was behind him so I could get a look at his ass, nice and flexed while he does that.

This has been going on all night and it's only getting worse. I want him. I need a drink. Thankfully, the cocktail waitresses abide. Fitting the occasion, I order a Vesper, and then a vodka martini when the waitress doesn't know what a Vesper is. Philistines.

Julian gets closer. I can feel him behind my head. I tilt back just a bit, and suddenly I'm touching his chin. He doesn't move for a moment, but then blinks and pulls away. I can see him in the mirror behind the table.

I play a few hands, win some, lose some, and gradually my focus fades. I'm tired, I'm buzzed, and Julian's presence is like tingling fingers dancing over my skin. When I stand up, the dealer stares straight at my crotch. I'm erect.

Julian follows as I head for the cashier to exchange my chips. He keeps looking at me.

Gradually it dawns on me that we've lost the others. Fuck.

"Where is everybody?" he says.

"Damned if I know," I say. "Let's look around."

Half an hour into the search, it occurs to me that they left without us. The fucks.

I snarl, gritting my teeth as my fists clench.

"They fucking left us behind," I snap.

"Shit," Julian mutters. "Did anybody tell you where they were going next?"

I shake my head. "I know as much as you do. They

probably planned on this. We were dragging them down. I swear if that little shit fucks around on my sister——"

Julian rests a comforting hand on my arm. "Easy, easy, big guy. I'm not best buds with Alex but he's a standup guy. He's not going to do anything stupid."

"I don't know," I growl. "The stupid strip club was already walking the line. He's getting married."

Walking with me for the exit, Julian muses, "I know, right? I get the joke of 'freedom' and all but some guys take it a little too seriously. If getting married is something you need to get drunk to commit to, maybe you ought to reconsider it, don't you think?"

I nod. "Yeah. I think."

"So, what do we do?"

"Work our way back to the hotel, I guess," I say. "Fuck it, I'm rich. I'll get us a limo."

Julian checks his phone. "Nobody will be back for hours. We can always go do something else."

There's a delectable lilt to his voice, and a subtle heat in his glance, as if he's testing the waters. Whether it's lust or a gambling high or liquid courage, he's throwing down the gauntlet.

I look over at him. "Good point. You're more interesting than I thought. I have an idea. Let's go downtown."

"Downtown?"

"Freemont. The real hardcore casinos. This bullshit is all tourist traps. Kids casinos."

I motion to the clothing boutiques inside the lobby. "I hate playing games in a fuckin' mall."

Taking his arm in my hand, I guide him over to the concierge's desk and bark orders for a limousine. When I flash my black card—made of a thin layer of stainless steel, not plastic—the woman at the desk jumps to do as I say.

I'm a bit of an asshole, but I have fun with it.

Not ten minutes later, there's a limo out front for us. I slip the driver a tip and tell him to take us downtown. This is no junior prom limo. Inside is lush and plush, like sinking into a big recliner. Julian climbs in after me and flops down next to me, a little woozy.

His head taps my shoulder as he starts to lean over, only to jerk back like he'd touched a hot stove.

"Sorry," he mutters.

"It's okay," I say, yawning.

Julian is staring at my crotch. For good reason. I'm hard as a rock. I trace my eyes down his body and find him aroused too, a nice bulge in his khaki shorts. The limo is absolutely crawling. I reach over and flick the button, raising the glass partition that obscures us from the driver.

Julian laughs quietly to himself.

"What?" I say.

"I was just thinking I'm glad we don't have a black light to shine in here. I bet this limo has seen some shit."

I laugh. "Like what?"

"I don't know," he says. "Haven't you ever been tempted to stand up in the sunroof of a limo?"

"And look like an idiot? I'd probably get us pulled over."

"Just stand up and yell 'I'm king of the world.' I dare you."

I reach over and open the sunroof. Baking Las Vegas air, that wonderful dry heat, comes blasting in like I'd opened the door to a furnace. Shakily, I stand up, rising through the opening.

It loses some of its effect when we're not moving. I glance down, ready to motion for Julian to stand next to me.

Except he's not. He's sitting on the floor of the limo.

He looks up at me with his big eyes and licks his lips. I plant my hands on the roof and stare at him. The moment builds, a silent pressure at the back of my skull. My dick is fucking throbbing. Playfully, Julian flips a single finger along the outline of my cock.

A shudder ripples through my entire body. He starts stroking me through my jeans.

"Stop it," I blurt. "I'm going to cream my fucking pants."

"Wouldn't want that to happen," he says, staring at my throbbing dick. "I wonder what would happen if I did this."

I almost stop him. My whole body is tingling, like I'm standing in a cold wind even though it's ninety-five degrees outside. Julian undoes my belt, loosens my pants and I gasp in shock as his cool fingers wrap around my shaft. He tugs and my dick comes loose, springing in his face. My balls fall out, dangling in front of him. He stares, wide-eyed.

"Holy fucking shit," he mutters.

This can't be happening. It can't be real.

It is. The world slows and I devour every second of this, savoring it. The feeling of his hand wrapped around my shaft. The air on my cock and balls. His hot breath before his lips make contact. They close lightly around the head and he presses forward, stroking me with those soft, pillowy lips, enveloping me. A hot urge, almost pain, tightens in my balls and legs and ripples into his mouth. I groan, then look around and realize I'm surrounded by people. If I sit down, he might stop.

Jesus Christ he's blowing me, and he's fucking good. No one has ever had this kind of skill with my dick. His mouth feels amazing, warm and hot, and his tongue strokes over my shaft. As he bobs his head, he takes me deeper, deeper, I hear him cough, he struggles...

Holy hell, his tongue is tickling my balls. They tighten up and I instinctively grab his head and keep my cock buried in his throat. When I look down and let go, he pulls back, my shaft still caught between his lips, and stares up at me, cheeks hollowed from sucking.

I'm in heaven. My legs are starting to buckle.

I sink back into the seat, dropping out of the sunroof. Julian crawls between my legs and goes back to work. I like it better this way. I stare, slack-jawed, like this is happening to someone else, crying out when the pleasure he gives ripples through my body. I let out a long, ungodly sound, half moan and half something else I don't even have words for, as I grasp his head in my hands. His hair tickles my fingers while I work my hips as he pumps his head.

I can't take very much of this. I'm going to explode. I moan something that sounds like a warning, and he ignores it. Somehow, he manages to smile with a mouthful of cock as I give him a mouthful of cum, exploding in the wet heat of his sucking lips. He plunges me down his throat and strokes more out with the muscles of his neck as he swallows, then draws back.

When he finally lets go and my cock sags in front of him, he grins. He hasn't spilled a single drop.

I hike my pants up, staring at him. He kneels patiently in front of me, hands resting on his thighs, an excited look on his gorgeous face as he gazes at me, grinning.

"You have no idea how long I've wanted to do that," he says.

I jerk forward. He yelps as I grab him and pull him on top of me. My hands fumble, then I have his pants open. I throw him on his back, push his knees apart, and grab his cock. I'm not used to this. I don't leap on it with the same eagerness he did when he took mine. He slouches in the seat and stares down at me.

Gingerly holding his shaft—he's bigger than I expected; skinny guys always seem to have the biggest dicks —I stare at it. I always thought this would feel submissive, but I have the power here. I've got him in my hands, as it were. What would it feel like to suck him off?

Let's find out.

CHAPTER 2

JULIAN

Oh my God. Oh my God.

Okay, first, my dream just came true. I sucked off Colton. He blew his load down my throat. I feel like I'm floating. Now he's got me on my back and he's got me in his hand. His skin is rough and hot as his palm and fingers curl around my shaft. Then...

Oh. Oh wow.

His lips wrap gingerly around my shaft and he sucks. I moan in ecstasy, a shudder rolling through my body as my fingers tighten on the limo seat. Colton sucks and bobs his head. He's new at this but he learns fast. I giggle like an idiot, laughing, only for my face to go slack with every fresh ripple of pleasure.

Damn me, why didn't I bring a condom? I need to be fucked so bad. My shoulders and neck call out for hands. My ass tightens as he sucks me, begging to be filled with cock. I want him to throw me down on the floor of this limo, face down, ass up, shove in me to the root, and make me take it. I want to feel his cock swell as he fills me up. Fuck it, I want him to grab my neck, slap my ass until it's raw, and make his little bitch call him daddy.

Oh god, this is embarrassing. I can't stop it. I cry out as a too-fast orgasm rips through me, all my jerk-off fantasies coming to life.

He's swallowing. This is really happening. Suddenly I'm on the floor with him and his tongue is in my mouth, all our tastes swirling together as his hands shove under my clothes. Colton spreads his fingers and grips my ass. When he squeezes, I yelp. His fingers tweak my nipples, reach up through my shirt and grasp my neck as he savages me with his mouth and tongue, kissing me like he wants to eat me like a little treat.

"Oh God I need you to fuck me," I moan.

He actually starts pulling my pants down.

Wow. Wow, he's hard again. Feeling his erection against my leg, I wonder if my eyes are too big for my ass, as it were.

"Condom," I sigh.

"You have one?" he says.

I shake my head.

"Get one," he says. "Get one, fuck the casinos."

He yanks his pants up, then mine, and pushes me back into the seat. We're both quivering like teenagers about to get laid for the first time when he cracks the partition down a little and says to the driver,

"Pull into the first drug store and wait."

He rolls it back up again. The limo turns off the Strip into the parking lot of a Walgreens. Colton leaps for the door. I grab his arm.

"Lube," I say. "We need lube."

He rushes out, then rushes back. His fucking hard cock is bouncing in his pants as he clambers back into the car.

He rolls the window down a little bit, again, and tells the driver,

"Drive. I don't care where, just drive until I tell you to stop."

When it's back up, I eye him. I can't keep my hands off him. His cock is in them again. I can barely get my fingers around it, and it's so long that both my palms can't cover it. I'm barely going to be able to take this thing.

"He has to know what we're doing," I say.

"Like I fucking care," he says, shoving my mouth onto his cock.

I can still taste his last orgasm. I stroke him to full hardness with my lips, fumbling with the condom wrapper. He doesn't even see me tuck it into my mouth, and stares at me as I slip him down my throat and rise, the condom nicely rolled down his shaft. I finish unrolling it and pat the tip of his cock lightly with my hand as if to say, good boy.

"I have to tell you something," I say, stroking his stomach.

"What?"

"I like it rough. Throw me down."

Then it's happening. I land on the limo floor with a thud, my knees under me, ass up. As Colton yanks my pants down so hard I hear a few stitches pop, I pull my knees forward, shoving my ass out even more. Air tickles my skin. Colton's jeans and belt clatter to the floor. He's stroking himself, wet noises as he lubes up his cock. A finger shoves into my body and I tense, feeling him spread the slickness.

For somebody who, as far as I knew before right now, was straight as an arrow, he sure knows how to get me ready. He works a second finger in, even spreads me a little, pumping his hand into my ass.

"Fuck," he growls, "I can't wait to feel this."

When he mounts me, it's like he tries to lunge over me. I make a groaning noise when the thick head of his dick presses into my asshole. It grows louder and higher in pitch as I open around him and higher still as his length slides into me. It feels like it'll go on forever and the sensation spikes until it chokes away my moan, leaving a silent hiss coming out of my throat.

I fucking love this part, when I first feel his size. I arch up and my back hits his chest and it's on. He thrusts and my whole body ripples with pleasure, building with pressure behind my cock and balls. I'm so hard it feels like I'll explode any second. I bite my lip and purr.

Colton falls on top of me, planting his hands on the floor beside mine, pressed into my back. Then he starts fucking me for real, slow at first, building speed and pressure and force with every stroke. I moan, loud and hot, too absorbed in my own pleasure to care if anyone can hear me.

A horn beeps outside and I shake with a start. I think someone honked at my moan.

Undulating and writhing under him, I savor the feeling of invasion, the thick heat of his shaft ravaging me. This is incredible, and we've already both come, so he can last as long as he wants.

I reach for my dick to stroke myself off, but Colton grabs my hand and pushes it down to the carpet. He holds his hands on top of mine and pins them, leaning over me until my chest touches the floor. I lay my cheek on it and take my fucking.

"You like that?" he growls in my ear.

"Yeah," I whimper, "I love it. Call me a bitch."

He flinches. I can feel it in his dick, even. He flares inside me as the ripple passes through his body and tenses muscles in his loins. I moan slightly and he presses his lips to my ear.

"Take my cock like a good little bitch."

I almost come just from that. Moaning in my ear, he thrusts even harder. I'm shaking all over, taken past the breaking point.

Colton rears up, grabs my ass in his hands, and pumps furiously. When he cuts loose, when the pleasure overtakes him and he doesn't care about even pretending to be gentle, it drives me so wild I don't care if it hurts. He buries deep, holds, and I feel the pulses of him coming inside me. I rise up on my hands and push back against him, holding him in me until my orgasm finishes.

Roughly, he flips me on my back, takes my cock in his mouth, and slides two fingers up my ass. My eyes roll back and close as the pleasure comes. When I finish in his mouth it almost hurts, it's so intense, even more than the first time.

Colton rears up and looks down at me. Lying on the floor of the limo with my knees out, my cock pulsing, and my shirt pulled up to my chest to bare my stomach, I feel like a submissive little bitch. My shivers aren't from the cold. This is so perfect. All my fantasies have come true. I want more.

"How many more are in the box?"

"Easy," he says, panting. "Aren't you sore?"

"I don't care," I say, rising up to run my hands up his chest under his shirt. "Fucking destroy my ass, Colton." I giggle like an idiot. "You don't know how long I've wanted to say that."

"Tell me," he says, breathless.

"I've wanted you to make me scream since I met you."

He grabs me. We kiss. His mouth is harsh, hints of teeth with tongue as he rubs against me.

Hurriedly, we arrange our clothes. Colton throws the used condom out the window.

"Hey," I yelp.

"It's not the only one," he says, "trust me."

I give him a sharp look. He rolls the window down just a touch.

"Drop us at a downtown casino," he says. "I don't care which, pick one."

The driver must be sending a message. He pulls up to the south entrance of a casino called, I kid you not, Big D's.

Yeah.

I stumble inside, sore ass and sore throat and all, drunk on sex. At the first table of craps, Colton pulls out more money than I make in a year and gets all black chips, hands half to me, digs his fingers firmly in my ass, and says, "Now, play just like daddy tells you."

The dealers give him some looks, but they look at his chips first and ignore it. I laugh like an idiot. Fuck them! I'm out and proud and I just had the best, roughest sex of my life with my lifelong crush. Fuck the world!

A cocktail waitress pops up, declaring her wares.

"Appletini," I blurt, "Make it a double!"

I drain it fast. We play. The chips flow. Colton just tells me what to do and I do it and in maybe an hour or so, I've won a month's pay from my freelancing work, then even more. I start getting paid in little rectangular chips instead of regular casino chips, and the people who work there look pissed. I get bad with my glamor pixie self, bouncing in place and clapping and fuck anybody who doesn't think I'm manly enough. Fuck the world.

Then I start my fourth appletini.

That's the last thing I remember for the night.

Morning light knifes into my eyeballs, waking me up by reminding me that everything I do is grotesquely stupid. Bellowing it in my ear. I fumble around on the hotel bed, wondering how the fuck I got here. As I look around, peeling my eyes open with my fingers to get those post-bender crusts out of my eyelashes, I spot condoms on the nightstand. Used condoms. My first impulse is to go, *ewww*.

My second impulse is to bark, out loud, "holy shit there's six of them. What the hell?"

Groaning, I slip off the bed. I'm sore. That's an under-statement. My mouth tastes like cock, applesauce, and bad liquor. I feel like I've been fucked by a bullet train. I lean over the nightstand and pick up my phone. I have eight missed calls from Karen and about fifty text messages from ten different people. Then I grab my wallet. It's stuffed so full of cash it won't close all the way. Hundred-dollar bills. I yelp, almost dropping it. I think I dreamed that in some booze haze. I'm rich! Ish. Rich-ish. A week's worth of rich.

It starts to dawn on me that it really happened. Like the real world rushing back in after rising from the deep sea of dreams, I begin to understand: I had sex with Colton. I glance at those condoms again. Sex with is an understatement. He fucked the living hell out of me. I'm probably lucky to be alive. His dick is an ICBM. An Inter-cockinental Butt-tastic Missile. A Weapon of Ass Destruc-tion. I look over at him. Yeah. It's real, he's actually there, lying on his back in all his perfectly muscled glory. I start towards him, all ready to fulfill my romantic fantasies of waking my boyfriend with a sloppy morning blowjob, and freeze.

You know what? My finger feels weird.

Staring at my hand in wonder, I realize, after a moment, that the gold band on my finger isn't a cheap knockoff novelty copy of Sauron's famous totem of power.

It's a plain gold band. There's only one reason people wear plain gold bands. Especially with engagement rings set with sapphires and a diamond that looks like it cost the gross domestic product of a small European country. What the fuck?

Colton groans and rolls over. As he moves, he reveals an envelope.

I tug it out from under him, open it, and slip out the paper inside.

It's…

Holy shit it's a marriage license. Because I'm married. To Colton.

I stare at the signatures, the form, all of it, in naked disbelief. Because I am naked. So is he. He sits up and the sheet slides away from his body, and wow. Okay. I married up.

"Colt," I say.

"What? Go 'way."

"Colt," I repeat.

"Why are you calling me that?"

"Dude, you jackhammered my ass all night, I'm giving you a pet name. Besides, look at this."

I hand him the paper. He stares at it lamely for a minute, then at his hand. He, too, wears a wedding band.

It takes him about as long to process it as it did for me.

"Wha?" he says. "What the fuck?"

"Uh," I say. "I do."

"I don't remember doing this," he says.

"Last thing I remember is appletini number whatever. I wish I could remember that," I point to the evidence of last night's debauchery.

He glances at it, then at me.

"Are you okay?"

"Yeah, I'm fine. Do you see what you have?"

"Yeah," he mutters. "This is a joke, right? We bought a novelty one."

I show him my rings. "These aren't a joke."

He looks at it. "Fucking hell, that's a real diamond."

"We. Got. Married," I say, breathless.

He looks at me in utter shock.

"Shit," he says, "shit shit shit."

"What?" my voice cracks.

He looks at me. "It's not that. I mean it is that. I can't get married, Julian. I can't be married. Not yet. You don't understand. My parents—"

"What?"

"If they found out I married a guy, they'd cut me off. Look, we can still...I need to get this undone before they find out. Take those rings off."

My heart sinks. I slip them off and offer them to him. There's a little mark on my finger anyway.

He grabs my shoulders. "Look at me. It's not like that. It—"

"COLTON!" Karen screams through the door, hammering it with her fists. "Are you in there? Where the hell is Julian? We have to leave for the airport in an hour! If you don't answer me, I'm calling the cops!"

"Fuck!" we both yelp at the same time.

He looks at me.

I look at him.

"Hide," he says.

Leaping to my feet, I grab my clothes—what I can find, anyway—and run for it. I don't know where to go. Bathroom, have to go to the bathroom.

Ducking inside, I crack the door. Colton yanks on shorts and struts to the door. When he opens it, Karen explodes into the room.

"Is he with you? Where is he? I can't find him."

"Why would he be with me?" Colton says, innocently. He scratches his chin at the same time.

I roll my eyes so hard it hurts. If that's the extent of his acting skills, we're screwed.

Karen stares at him.

"He was last seen with you," she says, eyes narrowing.

"Last seen with," Colton says. "You're talking about him like he disappeared."

"He did disappear! What do you think 'I can't find him' means, you big ox-headed muscle creature?"

He scowls at her. "Why are you asking me?"

She throws up her hands. "Jesus, I'm starting to think you buried him in the desert. Number one, like I fucking said, he was last seen with you. Trevor told me you two wandered off and got lost."

"Why aren't you yelling at Trevor?"

"Because it wouldn't do me any good. I might as well go yell at a package of bacon. Besides, number two, I told you to look out for him!"

My heart does a weird thing in my chest, half between skip and flutter. That's kind of romantic.

"Those idiots lost us," he protests.

"I don't care! When did you last see him?"

"Well," he says, his eyes screaming 'don't look at the ring on my finger,' "we went gambling and we were drinking and...I don't know. I think we...I blacked out."

Her jaw actually drops.

"Are you fucking kidding me? You took Julian out into Las Vegas, got him drunk, and lost him?"

"I...guess?"

"That's the opposite of looking out for him, you thundering *fucking* idiot. What the fuck am I going to do now? We're supposed to be in the Keys in twelve hours. Did you forget that I'm getting married? My best friend might have been abducted and sold to a drug cartel!"

"For what?"

"I don't know!" she screams.

Colton locks eyes with me and motions at the door. If I slip out and get past her, I can get to the door. Except I'm buck ass naked. I manage to grab my jeans, phone, one sock, and my wallet. Thankfully my wallet has my room key.

Oh shit, if Karen looks down, she'll see my shoes next to the bed. Shit, shit, shit.

Colton cocks his head to the side. Go, he seems to be saying. Go while she's distracted.

Uh. Shit.

I yank my jeans on, stuff my crap in my pockets, and ease out of the bathroom. It's a big room. I can slip past the bedroom to the door if I take it slow. Don't turn around. Don't turn around. Don't turn around.

Somehow, I manage to get past her to the door, slide it open, and retreat into the hallway. Karen has gone full Karen, unleashing the hounds of hell on her poor sweet handsome delectable man-slab of a brother.

One-socked and sticky in my jeans, I sprint down the hall, fumble, and get into my room. Shit, shit, shit. I need to let her know I'm okay.

I grab the phone and dial Colton's room.

Karen bellows "What?" into the phone so loud I can hear her voice both in the handset and in Colton's room down the hall.

"What?" I repeat back, lamely.

"Julian?" she says. "Where are you?"

"Uh, in my room," I say.

I probably should have had a plan before I picked up the phone.

"What? I pounded on the door for fifteen minutes. I almost called the cops!"

"I'm fine, sorry. Hard night last night, you know? Partied hard."

"Colton was supposed to watch out for you."

He fucked me until I almost can't walk. "Oh, he did, he was great."

"Did he bring you back here?"

"Oh yes, he did. He even got us a limo. He's very sweet, Karen."

She makes an annoyed noise. "You two, I swear. We have to catch a plane! Hurry up, you've got maybe fifteen minutes before the shuttles pick us up."

She's still yelling at Colton as she slams the receiver down.

Hurry up.

It's like moving underwater. The sheer enormity of it all. The situation. The implications. His penis. All enormous.

I'm a little sad that I don't remember my wedding. A little heartbroken he wants to undo it. A little excited he said we can still…actually, he didn't say what we can still, I hope he wasn't about to say, "be friends."

Internal. Screaming.

I plunge into a hot shower, clean myself as best I can, and leap out, rushing through the room to do two hours of packing in ten minutes. When I have all my crap stuffed haphazardly into my bags, I rush for the door. I don't know what happened to my other sock, my underwear, or my shirt, and I don't have time to find out. We're off to paradise for my best friend's destination wedding.

As soon as I step out of the elevator, everyone looks at me. I'm sure it's because Karen made a scene looking for me and not because everyone on both sides of the aisle and in the wedding party knows that Colton went through two boxes of condoms in my butt. I sheepishly avoid him, shying close to Karen. She sniffs the air and motions us all forward to the waiting shuttles.

Off we go. Paradise bound.

You'd think my husband would sit next to me. I pile into the van and—

Bethany is staring straight at me, her lips pressed together in a thin line that might be a smirk or might be fury, I don't know.

"I hope it was worth it," she says.

"Huh?"

"Your good time last night," she says, calmly. "Almost had us all late."

She flubs the T a little, like she meant to say, "laid."

Oh God, she—

Julian! I shout at myself, silently. Enough. They're not psychic, they don't know what happened, chill out and carry on.

Alright, alright. Keep a clear head, Julian. Let's get through security.

At the airport, we're one of those obnoxious clans of people all on the same flight. Security at McCarran airport is a breeze and the screeners are a jovial sort. After submitting to the humiliation of the body scanner, the whole group moves towards the gate. I'm pretty sure that Karen basically booked all of us first class on the flight.

This was a long trip ahead of us. Flight to Miami-Dade and then to Key West. Bleh.

Colton catches my eye and nods his head. It takes a few nods before I catch on that he's trying to signal me to follow him. He casually splits off from the group and heads over to a Cinnabon, pulling his bag behind him.

I catch up with him a moment later.

"What took you so long?" he says.

"I'm trying to be covert."

"Nobody is going to see us," he says. "What are you doing?"

I was getting in line to order something.

"Getting a bun. Want some buns, Colt?"

"No," he growls, "and stop calling me that. We need to talk."

"Sure, hubby."

"Julian!"

His voice is just loud enough to catch some looks from random passengers. A passerby with a green Mohawk gives us a knowing look. As spectacles go, we must be pretty run-of-the-mill for Las Vegas, but I'd rather not cause a scene.

I sigh, wandering away from the pastry place with him.

"We have to get the marriage annulled," he says.

I sigh again. Loudly. He glares at me.

"Don't pout. Look…let's just get that out in the open. We're not staying married, if that thing is even legally binding. By the way, where is it?"

"Oh, the marriage license? I have it."

His eyes narrow. "Hand it over."

"It's safe with me."

He bites his lip and glares down at me.

"Fine, fine, you can have it," I say. "Want it now?"

"Yeah."

I rummage around in my messenger bag, find it, and hand it over. He slips the envelope in his suitcase.

"It takes both people to get the marriage annulled," he says.

"Yeah, yeah, I know."

"I want to take care of it after the wedding."

He looks at me.

"So," I say, indignant. "Wham, bam, thank you man?"

"I'm not ready to get married," he says. "We spent one night together, and we were both drunk off our asses."

I take a step closer to him and force my voice low. It turns into a shrill hiss. "Last night was everything I ever wanted."

A vein pulses on his neck. He's looking at me hard, his eyes boring into my essence, deep diving into my soul.

"You barely know me. I don't know if this is some kind of crush or something, but we don't know each other at all."

"So? Let's get to know each other," I say, resting my hand on his chest.

He grabs my wrist. "Not in public."

"Why not?"

"Well, my parents might see us, for one thing," he says, his voice a dangerous growl. "Look, it may be all well and good for you in Seattle being out and proud, but my family is old money. If they were to tolerate me...having a...you," he says, stumbling over the words, "it'd have to be covert, and I'm still expected to get married and have a kid."

I eye him, frowning.

I don't know if he knows this or not. It would be odd if Karen told me, but not her brother. I don't want to be the one to break the news. Maybe it's her last spark of her upbringing holding her back, but she confided in me that she didn't want to announce that she's pregnant until she gets married. She's not showing or anything yet, but she's sure. She went to a doctor and everything. I know, I was there.

If Colton is worried about producing an heir for the family or whatever, he's got it covered. I chew my lip, tucking it under my front teeth.

"Please stop doing that," he says.

"Doing what?"

"The lip bite thing."

"Why?" I say, brushing my hair back from my face. "Does it turn you on?"

"I said, stop it."

"Whatever you say, daddy."

"Jesus Christ," he barks, "Do not do that in public."

"How about in private? You liked it last night."

"I barely remember last night."

"I remember enough," I counter. "I don't want to be somebody's side piece."

"Maybe it doesn't have to be something serious," he says, studying me. "We've got a few days together, and nobody is going to be paying attention to where either of us is until the newlyweds get back from their euro-tour…"

I scowl. "Seriously. Listen to yourself. 'Hey Julian, you're a great fuck but I seriously need to get our marriage annulled, oh and by the way, I'd like to keep banging you in secret.' You are too fucking much, Colt."

"Stop. Calling. Me. That."

I stick out my tongue.

"You're just being childish," he says.

"I'm not a little bitch," I hiss.

"You liked it when I called you that last night."

We stare at each other.

"Look," he says. "I need time. This is new for me. I've never been with a…you, before. I thought I was, you know."

"Straight," I say. "But you're not. Congratulations, you found your bi-card in my butt."

"Gah," he says.

"You liked it when you were hip deep."

"Can we stop saying that?" he snaps.

"Fine," I huff. "Okay. I'll annul the marriage, but I want you to give me a real chance."

His eyebrows rise. "Are you blackmailing me?"

"I'm not after your money," I say.

He cocks his head. "You know, if you're blackmailing me for sex, that's probably worse. Ethically."

"Oh, fuck you," I mutter.

"I know that's your plan."

"Pfft."

"This is getting out of hand," he says, scrubbing both hands through his hair.

"You'll only be getting it in hand if you don't watch yourself."

"You're impossible."

"You're impossible," I throw back at him. "Why don't you just give it a chance? I like you. You like me. We had a great time last night. It doesn't have to stop over some bull-shit from your parents. Be your own man."

He grits his teeth. "I don't like it when people say that to me."

"There's so much about you I always wanted to know," I offer, softening my tone. "Look, I'm giving you what you want. No strings attached. I'm asking, not demanding, that you give me a chance. We need to get back before everyone notices we're both missing."

He nods. "Right, right."

The whole way to the gate, butterflies swirl in my stomach. Then acid-spitting attack beetles start savaging the butterflies. By the time we actually get there, I think there's a nature documentary freaking out in my esophagus. I'm going to throw up.

Now I have to strap into a giant metal tube that rides on exploding chemicals at hundreds of miles an hour at an altitude of six miles.

Yeah.

CHAPTER 3

COLTON

He didn't sit next to me, and I don't know how I feel about that. It was by design; Karen set up all the seating on the plane and put Julian with herself, near the front. Our parents are way in the back.

She put me next to Trevor and she did it on purpose. Our cousin smells like ten cheap beers gangbanged a steak sandwich. It's worse when he belches, which is early and often. I end up going to the bathroom ten times during the long leg of the flight, not to relieve myself in the usual sense but to be free of the stench. I sit on the airplane toilet until someone bangs on the door and forces me out. The plane lavatory smells better than my cousin.

Besides that, he's just offensive to look at. He somehow chooses clothing that clashes with his skin, itself, and the concept of human decency. Today he's wearing two polo shirts, a pink one over a banana yellow one, with both collars popped and wraparound shades which remain perpetually perched in his spiky hair but nevertheless leave tan lines on his face, like a shadow reversed in a photographic negative.

God, I hate him.

He won't shut up, either. He drones constantly to everyone around him or to anyone or anything in range or to himself if no one is paying attention, which is often. Unfortunately, someone switched seats with the groom's friend Jordan, meaning that I've already lost four hours of my life to the pair of them comparing, describing, and rating each pair of breasts they saw in Las Vegas. Hunched up against the window in fear that Trevor's scent will permeate my flesh, I try my best to tune them out.

Finally, four hours into the flight, I've had enough.

"Will you two please shut the fuck up," I snarl, louder than I planned. Loud enough that half the first class seats either crane forward or turn around to see what's going on and alleviate the boredom of flight. Once you get used to it, plane travel is basically riding in a really loud, smelly, cramped bus.

Trevor turns to me slowly, the wheels visibly spinning in his head. I can see him deciding whether to bro-out and challenge me to a bro-down or back off and close his disgusting mouth. I don't think he even brushed his teeth. By the smell of him he simply blasted his entire body with body spray and changed his clothes.

I meet his gaze levelly. "Well?"

"Dude, what's your problem?"

"Being stuck in a flying metal cylinder with you for another six hours."

I actually start to stand up, but with the overhead bin above my seat I don't have much room to rise. Trevor unbuckles his belt, no doubt planning a "hold me back, hold me back" display of machismo I have absolutely zero tolerance for.

"Hey!" Karen barks, her voice cutting through the din.

I swear, she should have been a kindergarten teacher. She can control a room with just her voice.

A hand taps my shoulder. It's Alex, my sister's husband-to-be.

"Hey man, why don't we switch seats for a bit."

I nod and clamber out from the pit of Cheeto-flavored despair, relieved to be away from them. Until I spot the seat that Alex vacated for me.

Julian is against the window. I'll be taking the aisle. Karen will be right in between us.

Well, shit.

I settle into the seat and adjust myself. Karen, arms crossed, fumes. Julian slowly, very carefully, turns his head just enough to catch my eye and snaps his head forward, his Adam's apple bobbing as he swallows hard.

"Uh," he says.

Karen glances at him. "Huh?"

"Nothing," Julian chirps.

She turns to me. Angrily.

"Can you please not cause a bro-battle at my wedding?"

"We're not at the wedding yet," I growl.

"Come on. I know you had soooo much to do," she says, dragging the word out to hang it around my neck, "but you can deal for a few hours."

"I've had to put up with those idiots for a week, and you don't like them either."

"That's not the point," she hisses. "This is my wedding. It's not about you."

I huff and immediately regret it even as I fold my arms. It's like putting us in the same room regresses me to twelve and her to six, when she was throwing a tantrum to get some of the attention our parents heaped on me. I wouldn't wish their attention on my enemy, but if I tell her that, she'll just blow up at me. Again.

"Let me give you a little sample of what I've listened to for the last four hours, Karen. 'Hey bro, who had the biggest tits?' 'The redhead!' 'No, she didn't those were bee stings man!' 'No, the other red head!' 'Nah man, she wasn't a redhead, carpet didn't match the drapes!' 'Like you fuckin' know!' 'Champagne room, bro'!'"

"Alright, alright," Karen says. "I get it."

"You haven't gotten the full experience," I say. "Here. Bro. Bro. Bro bro bro? Brobro, brobrobro, brobrobrobro-brobrorborborborborborbor…"

"I GET IT," Karen bellows, again, turning every head in the front section of the plane.

Julian plunges his face in his hands and hides.

"Back me up here," I say to him.

He snaps up and looks at me, eyes wide, and gives me a little shake.

Karen's head whips back and forth.

"Don't tell me you two bonded," she says.

"Uh, no," Julian protests. "I've barely talked to him. He's got a point, though." He lowers his voice. "They can be really obnoxious."

Karen huffs. "I don't even like them. That's not the point."

"You said that," I offer, smoothly. "Then what is the point?"

"The point is…I don't even know. Can we just sit here until we land?"

I slink down in my seat, kick it back, and ready myself to go to sleep. "Sure," I say and close my eyes.

My head hurts anyway. Every time I move it feels like reality is on a split-second delay, and I hear a faint rubbery sound every time I move my neck. I probably drank enough booze last night to kill a bull elephant. I'm probably lucky Julian didn't barf on me.

Hell, maybe he did and I cleaned him up and I don't remember.

Eventually, somehow, I drift off to sleep.

When I wake up, it's because the plane dropped ten feet. Karen yelps, and even Julian mutters something. We must have hit turbulence. The seatbelt sign is on.

"Ladies and gentlemen, this is your captain speaking. We're about two hours out from Miami-Dade International. It looks like we've hit a little bit of a low-pressure zone coming up ahead. I've gone ahead and turned on the fasten seatbelt sign. Please remain seated for the time being."

As if to punctuate his declaration, the plane yaws from side to side, then turns as if a giant hand grasped the tail and torqued it to the right. Julian sits up straight as an arrow and hisses in a breath through clenched teeth. Karen grabs his hand.

"We'll be okay," I blurt out, without thinking.

Karen glances my way, utterly confused at the prospect of me comforting her, especially since she wasn't that concerned. I'm sure the two of us have logged more miles than almost anyone on the plane except our parents and the flight crew. My parents own several of their own planes; the only reason we're on this one is that none of the others are large enough.

Julian grabs the barf bag from the seat in front of him. He looks a little green.

Karen and I suddenly lock on to each other in thought: Please don't puke.

The plane does another abrupt, unplanned maneuver. The pilot comes on again.

"Flight attendants, please stow the service carts and buckle seatbelts."

Julian looks a little panicked.

"What does that mean?"

"Nothing," I say. "They just don't want to get sued when one of those little Coke cans smacks some toddler in the head."

Karen laughs, but it has a nervous tinge to it. Her fingers are white on the arm rests. I glance at her.

Ugh, such a pain being the strong one. My guts are turning to water. Why did I drink so much last night?

Julian is shaking a little.

"You okay?" I ask him.

He nods, sharply.

"He's fine," Karen snaps.

"Relax, I wasn't implying anything."

Scowling, she stares down at her feet.

"Karen, we're not teenagers anymore. Can we just act our age? I was legit worried. Not everything has to be a goddamn contest."

"Easy for you to say," she whispers so softly I doubt even Julian heard it.

I lean back in my seat and ignore her sally. Better not to keep it going. Be the bigger man, Colton.

The plane dives and the pilot hits the throttle. Someone screams. Julian almost jumps out of his seat and shoves his face into the barf bag at the same time. Karen even grabs hers.

"Fucking destination wedding," she snarls.

"Wasn't my idea."

"Mine either, lummox," she snaps.

"Look, we'll be fine. I've been in worse than this."

"You have?" Julian says, his voice warbling.

"Don't you know what I did in the navy?"

"No," he says. "Karen just said you were deployed."

"I was a fighter pilot. I landed on aircraft carriers."

He stares at me, wide-eyed.

Oh great, now it's hero worship.

"It's not a big deal," I mutter.

Karen looks at me, side-eyed. "Since when is it ever not a big deal? To hear Dad tell it you didn't just fly jets, you invented them."

"You've been through worse?"

"Couple bad scrapes, thought I was dead and gone," I say. "Had to do a few landings on instrumentation only. That was hairy."

"Instrumentation?"

"Flying blind, basically. Relying on the controller and instruments to land a really big jet on a very small air craft carrier in the middle of a very dark ocean on a very dark night in a nasty rain storm. This is a walk in the park next to that. Oh, what a lovely day."

Julian smiles, mollified.

As if banished by his calm, the turbulence abates. Eventually, the pilot even gives the all-clear for beverage service.

"Hair of the dog," I mutter, ordering a neat scotch.

It's neat but it barely qualifies as scotch. It smells like turpentine and tastes like nail polish remover with brown food coloring, but it eases the pounding in my head enough to make the cramped conditions tolerable.

"Do you still fly?"

Julian asked me. I turn my head without lifting it from the head rest.

"Yeah," I sigh.

"Do you have a plane?"

"Yeah," I say. "A couple."

He stares at me in naked fascination, and the look on

his face makes me picture him naked. I've seen that look on lots of women. The phrase fighter plot is basically a sorcerous incantation to make panties vanish into the panty dimension, but it's a little odd seeing it on a man's face.

Odd, and somehow more genuine. I actually get annoyed with the groupies, but it's endearing when Julian looks at me that way.

"You should take me flying sometime," he says.

Karen tenses, glancing at him.

"You'd have to sit on my lap."

Stupid, stupid, stupid. Don't drink.

Karen clears her throat. "Don't make fun of him, Colton."

I hate it when she ends a sentence with my name, like she thinks she's mom. She's sounded like my mother since she was six years old. Don't do this, Colton, don't do that, Colton. Colton, Colton, Colton. I get sick of hearing it.

Finally, we're coming in for a landing. Of course, we flew against the clock, so that even though it's still light out, it's late in the evening. Good, I'm glad to have skipped most of this day. I need sleep. Real sleep. I feel like I slept, but didn't rest last night. The time just disappeared.

Julian groans as the plane leans back to land.

He's white as a sheet until the wheels touch down. Only when they're all on solid earth again does he relax. Karen blows her hair out of her face.

"Layover," she says. "Remember? Two-hour flight to the Key."

"Euuugh," Julian says, stretching out the syllable like old gum.

"My sentiments exactly."

Hurriedly, I rush from my seat and grab my bag. Trevor is holding a grudge, I can see. He scowls.

"Go back to flavor town," I mutter, dragging my bag from over his head.

In the jetway, the oppressive, humid Florida heat reminds me that out in Vegas it really is dry, and I prefer it. Walking into the terminal feels like having rolled wax paper jammed up my nose. Hauling my bag with me, I meander to the group, avoiding Trevor as much as I can just to avoid the smell.

He's got that look. He wants to throw down. Fucking idiot. He's never been in a real fight in his life. It takes every ounce of concentration I have not to go over there and bop him on the nose. Not hard enough to do any lasting damage, just bleed him a little. Guys like him act the way they do because nobody ever stops them.

I can't stand that.

Julian keeps looking at me. We don't have time to really separate. If I follow him off again, someone will notice. My phone chirps.

He texted me.

What?

I text back, how did you get this number?

He replies: *Honestly, I don't remember. It's just in my phone. Are you really a fighter pilot?*

Was a fighter pilot, I send back.

I'm too hung over to come up with a good joke. Want to fire your missile into my exhaust?

Not now, I text back.

So, later?

Stop it.

You stop it.

Karen peeks toward my phone. I hastily put it away.

"Keeping secrets?" she says.

I glare at Julian over her head. I'm a good foot taller than my sister. I glance down as if I'd just noticed her.

"I have a life, too."

"You're probably on Tinder trying to set up a little MILF hunt on the Key," she says, voice dripping with disdain.

"No," I say. "I'm on that Bumble app. All I have to do is put in fighter pilot and you can hear the panties getting soaked in the next county."

She glares at me. "Can you have a little class?"

"Not if I want to fit in with this wedding party," I say, smoothly.

Karen opens her mouth and snaps it shut, either too tired or too wise to retort and get into this here. Alex swoops in and leads her away, glaring at me. Her husband's hand wanders a little too low and my throat tightens, heat rising from my collar.

Julian, watching all this, texts me again.

What was that about?

More of the same.

Ugh, we have to sit here for two hours.

I put my phone away, but as I do so, he sends another one.

Let's sext, it reads.

I send back, *No. I don't want a boner in the airport.*

Julian isn't giving up. *You make me such a slut, Daddy.*

I roll my eyes. *Trying too hard. Preserve some of the mystery. Be seductive.*

Oh, so now you want me to sext you?

I shove my phone in my pocket and glare at him, pointedly ignoring his next few texts until he angrily gives up and shoves his phone back in his jeans. I walk over to a bank of seats and flop down, waiting for the plane.

When I see it roll up, I groan. It's what my father always calls a puddle jumper, barely big enough to accommodate our whole group. The whole plane is probably booked for us. Julian stares at me until I read his latest text. I scroll through a stream of offers to suck my dick to a more serious one.

Are we flying on that? It has propellers.

They're called turboprops, I send back. *It's fine.*

He swallows and goes over to sit near, but not next to, Karen. My sister has been swarmed by her other bridesmaids.

Apparently, Julian is "Man of Honor" or something. He must really be close to Karen to suffer that kind of humiliation. I guess it's no weirder than best man. At least they're not calling him a maid.

Unbidden, I picture him in a slutty maid outfit. I almost text that to him but stop myself.

What the fuck are you doing, Colton? This can't go on. You have to send him back to Seattle and go on with your life. What's next, a dick pic?

The short layover means we start boarding after less than an hour and a half. There is no first class on a puddle jumper, just seats, and, as I suspected, it's all us. This isn't even all the guests, others will be flying in, or have flown in already.

Julian looks at me, following me with his gaze as I walk past on the plane. When I sit I already have an annoyed text waiting for me.

Rather sit with Flavortown than with me?

How did you know I call him that?

I guess we have something in common.

My sister can't know about this. She'll freak.

She knows I'm gay, dude.

Not the point. Doesn't matter if you're gay, all she's going to see is her hated brother plowing her best friend.

She doesn't hate you, Colt.

Stop calling me that.

He sends back a string of emojis, one of which is an eggplant. Whatever. I shove the phone in my pocket, lean back, and somehow manage to nearly sleep through take off. The flight is short—up and then back down again, almost in a parabola.

I jolt awake for the landing. It's nearly dark now. At the airport, there's no jetway. We descend stairs onto tarmac.

Key West is gorgeous, and the air has that ocean breeze feel that takes the edge off everything. I feel like I can breathe for the first time since we left Vegas. There's shuttles waiting to take us to the hotel.

We can go out tonight, Julian texts.

I want to sleep, I text back.

I can sneak into your room.

I need to think, I send back.

Think with me, he replies.

Annoyed, I stuff the phone back in my pocket and clamber into the shuttle. It's a short ride to the hotel— the island isn't that big—and then we're inside. The place is gorgeous, a low slung palatial vista that pulls off the kind of ostentation the Las Vegas gaucheries can only try and fail at. The very air fills me with longing for a straw hat and linen suit and a Hemingway novel. I wonder if Julian has ever been to see Hemingway's estate, with the cats.

What am I thinking? Of course not.

Finally, finally I am in my room. First, I pour myself into the shower and stand under the water until the rubbery feeling of two airplanes is gone, along with that disgusting airplane cleaner smell and the faint memory of an odor of my cousin. When I step out, there's a knock at the door, almost as soon as my heel hits the tile.

Without thinking, I open the door and Julian invites himself in.

"What are you doing here?" I demand, slamming the door shut.

Whatever he was going to say is lost as he stares at me.

"You're very wet. Muscles. Wet muscles."

His hair is damp; he must have showered, too. I can smell him. Every cell of my body urges me to sweep closer, grab him, and take in the scent of his wet hair before I throw him on the bed and rip off his fresh t-shirt and jeans.

"I said," I repeat, more slowly, "What are you doing here?"

He flops back on the bed and crosses his arms under his head. "I'm bored."

"We're not fucking."

"Don't worry, I'm ready for another round."

"I'm not," I say, angrily.

"What's the matter?" he says. "Afraid you'll wear me out?"

I huff. "No. We need to talk. Rules."

"Rules?" he says. "Oh, I like rules. That's one of my favorite kinds of play."

"This is serious," I say.

He lifts an eyebrow. "Maybe you should make me take it seriously."

"I will, by dragging you out of here and throwing your ass in the pool."

He laughs. "Oh, that'd make a big scene for Mom and Dad, wouldn't it?"

I fume. "Don't threaten me with that."

"Okay, okay," he says. "I was joking."

"You're really bold all of a sudden."

He sits up. "I think taking your dick down my throat a few times entitles me to a little familiarity. Don't you?"

His arrogant tone and the look on his sexy, handsome

face almost makes me grab him right there, but I stop myself. He rakes his eyes down my stomach to the tent forming under my towel. Angrily, I rush behind a screen to pull on a pair of jeans.

"Aww," he says. "Okay, okay. What are the rules?"

"It's a week," I say. "Then we're done."

He frowns but doesn't answer.

"My parents, and Karen, do not find out."

He nods.

"That means no one else does, either. We're on a small island here."

"Funny she picked the gayest island in the known universe," Julian declares. "This place has more queer per square inch than anywhere else in the world."

I flinch, and he catches it.

"What? Did I say something wrong?"

"Queer. That's a slur."

"Not if we use it."

"We?" I say.

"Sorry," he says. "You're bi now. Maybe even...gasp... gay. Maybe I'm so sexy you're only gay for me."

I gulp and tamp down my feelings. No, this isn't the first time I've been attracted to a guy...god, he might be right, I never felt anything like I felt last night when I was with women. Last night feels like another planet. Fucking jet lag.

"Are you okay?" he says. "You're staring at me. If we're going to go, let's go. Let me grab some lube and condoms."

"What?"

"I got them in the airport. You can't watch me every second."

"That's not what I mean. Go back to your room and go to sleep, Julian."

"I should have asked for adjoining rooms."

"Do not play games with me," I say, coolly.

"Where's the fun in that?" he says, stalking for the door. He carefully checks the peep hole, looks over his shoulder saucily at me, and ducks out into the hall, closing the door behind him.

I look down. Damn it, this isn't going away on its own.

I shove my jeans off and lay back on the bed, stroking myself. I cannot think of anything but Julian and the way it felt when his ass cheeks squeezed around my dick and swallowed me. I've never come that hard in my life, not even the first time when I finally figured out how to rub it right. Not even after going nearly three weeks the first time I was shipboard.

Fuck. I need another shower.

I take a longer one this time and crawl into bed nude.

Sleep is like flipping a giant switch that upends the universe. I didn't even eat dinner, and of course I'm famished. Karen's schedule gave everyone a day to get over the jet lag before the wedding proper. More activities. From this morning on, the pair are observing the old tradition about seeing the bride before the wedding, down to having separate rooms.

First, I slide out of bed and pull on a pair of jeans, throw on a shirt, and put my sneakers on without socks. Something about the air here leads everyone to gravitate outside. The hotel houses more than just the wedding guests, so continental breakfast is crowded. My head is still pounding, my tongue feels like there's mushrooms growing on it, and my eyes hurt.

The breeze is nice. The sun is too damn bright. I shuffle along awkwardly until I can spoon some eggs out of a steamer tray, grab some waffles with tongs, and find a place to stand up and eat, looking around everywhere.

Julian is with Karen, laughing as they talk about whatever. Probably soothing her nerves or cold feet. I almost start towards them, but stop. She won't be interested in seeing me right now. To say the least. Julian, though, notices me, a quick, startled glance like he hasn't seen me in years.

Maybe the change of venue has made him realize that yeah, that actually happened. I have the papers from the wedding in a suit jacket in my room. Yeah, that really happened.

I should be able to go over and sit with my sister. I wish I knew what I did to piss her off so much. She stares daggers at me constantly, trying to burn a hole in my skin. When she bothers looking at me at all.

Our parents are surrounded by the other older guests. Makes me wonder if they did something to her while I was away. I started school when she was twelve and went into the military when she was sixteen. When I came back, she'd moved to the other side of the country with her friend and started a new life. I honestly don't know why she even wanted to do all this, she never seemed like the bridezilla type.

Of course, if you looked around you'd think that her... friend Bethany was the bride, with all the women circling around her like an overly tanned queen holding some kind of Jersey Shore court. I really hope I don't get roped into some dumb group activity today. Last thing I feel like is parasailing or whatever it is people do here. I'd rather slink off, maybe see if I can find a bar.

My hands are shaking. My little sister is getting married tomorrow, I had sex with her best friend, and my life is turning upside down. Having taken only a few bites, I scrape my plate into a garbage can and walk away from the open dining area, looking for a way out into the open.

I need some air.

CHAPTER 4

JULIAN

"Have you seen my brother?"

Alarm bells go off in my head. That's an understatement. The inside of my head looks like the bridge of a starship—the 90's version where there's no seatbelts and a Frenchman with an English accent says, "make it so," and everything is vaguely similar to the interior of a Plymouth Voyager. Inside, klaxons are going off, red lights are flashing, and the crew are getting tossed around by proton torpedoes.

"Oh, I don't know, why would I have seen him?" I chirp, a little shrilly.

Karen gives me an odd look. "I don't know, because we're staying in the same hotel? What's up with you?"

"Nothing," I say. "Just jet lagged."

She leans forward. "Julian, I'm not dumb."

My hair almost stands on end. I swallow, hard, trying to run through as many possible ways as I can conceive to explain myself. You see, Karen, I wasn't planning to fuck your brother…well I was, but I didn't think he would. It was an accident. I totally didn't mean to suck his dick. I just tripped and boom, next thing you know, he's climaxing in my throat. Funny how that kind of thing happens, right?

"I have no idea what you mean," I say coolly.

She sighs and gives me a flat look.

"You have a crush on him. It's so obvious, Julian. You might as well have tried to suck his dick on the plane."

"What?" I say. "I did not."

"Oh, Colton you're so brave," she says in a sing-song voice, "You can land on my flight deck annyyyyy time. It's lame, Julian."

I frown.

"Look," she says, resting her hands on my shoulders. "Let's not fight, okay? I'm not saying it's wrong to feel the way you do. I'm sure my brother is to you what my posters in my room were to me, but he's really here, in flesh and blood. He's bad news. He'd just hurt you…if he was interested, which I can guarantee you he's not. He's a port-in-every-girl kind of guy."

He's not interested. He was totally disinterested in me when he used up two boxes of rubbers, Karen.

I sigh as if she's letting me down gently.

"Besides, he's my brother. It would be weird. I don't know who I'd be more disappointed in. Mostly him."

"Not for a lack of trying on her part," I say, sighing.

"Yeah. Don't get jealous, she's got no chance. The bottle blonde thing doesn't really work for Colton, believe me. He has a thing for brunettes."

Like me, I want to add, but don't.

After we grab breakfast, he appears.

I spot him first. Karen turns to see what I'm staring at and scowls.

"Could you stop?" she says, and I can't tell if the snap

in her voice is from heat or a joke. "I'm getting sick of picking your tongue up off the floor."

"Sorry," I mutter, turning. "You were looking for him."

"Yeah. I don't know why. Have I mentioned that I think this whole thing is dumb and I don't want to do it?"

My heart seizes. "What, get married?"

"All this," she says, waving her fork about. "I'd just as soon go sign some papers. I don't even know why we made it official. I was fine just living in sin."

Cold feet. It's a big decision and a huge life change. It's normal to be nervous.

Karen props her chin on her fist and stirs her food listlessly. "He pretty much sprung it on me. The proposal."

"I know," I say.

I felt a little off about that from the start, but I didn't say anything. Hell, I don't want to say anything now. It's not my place at all. Karen is an adult and can make her own decisions. Still...

Big, splashy public proposal. Lots of eyes and pressure to say yes, and her parents were there, as were his.

It's natural to feel pushed into something like that.

My eyes drift away from her. Colton has left the patio. I start itching to follow, but Karen is talking.

"Should I do this?" she says.

I blink a few times. "What, eat a waffle?"

"Get married," she sighs. "I already hate it here. Isn't this supposed to be fun?"

"Before the ceremony?" I say. "Probably not."

"You are so lucky you don't have to worry about this."

"Hey, I can get married, too," I point out.

"You've never talked about it," she says, shrugging.

"Um."

"What?"

"Nothing," I cough. "This is normal. Jitters the day

before. It's like a final exam or something. It's natural to be nervous, okay? You'll do fine."

"I hate being the center of attention."

"It'll all be over soon. Once the party starts, you can just let Alex handle all the attention-centering. Then a few days from now, you two are on your own and you get a nice vacation before you go back to getting out at work. Win-win for everybody."

"You're right," she says. "I just have this nervous feeling that something terribly weird has happened and I can't see what it is."

I swallow. "Right. Just nerves. Like when you keep thinking you left the stove on but it's because you forgot your purse."

"Yeah," she sighs.

She does that a lot. She has to keep little lists everywhere and an itinerary on her phone to keep things straight. Laser focused when she's working, but she'd forget to eat lunch if I didn't remind her half the time.

"Sigh," I say.

"You're supposed to actually sigh. Not just say sigh," she says.

"Sadface," I say.

"If you start pronouncing emojis again I'm going to change the seating at the reception so you're between Jordan and Trevor."

I shudder.

Karen looks concerned. "How did they treat you? I was in such a rush yesterday, I never asked."

"It sucked," I say. "I uh, don't have a lot in common with those guys."

"Yeah," she says. "It sounded like a boring night. Alex said you guys went to some dumb arcade bar and then spent the rest of the night gambling."

I shudder. "He did?"

"Isn't that what you did?"

"Yeah, sure," I blurt before I can think.

Did he…did they not tell her about the strip club? Is that normal? I have no idea if it is or isn't. I don't know how these kinds of things are supposed to work. Does the bride get to know where the bachelors went? Besides, nothing happened. Alex didn't even…

Wait, wasn't he alone with the strippers?

Shit, I didn't even do my damn job. I was so worried about hopping on Colton's dick that I forgot about the favor my best friend asked of me. Shame ripples under my skin, like the crawling limbs of invisible spiders.

"Well, that's good," she sighs. "We got a little wild. You'd have had a good time. We went to a couple of bars and then played laser tag."

"Yeah. I'd rather have been with you," I say, lying.

"I should see if I can find Colton," she says, rising. "I want to talk to him. Smooth things over a bit. Make sure he behaves at the wedding."

"I get you," I say.

"Then I've got the hair dresser and all that crap. You coming?"

"Uh, yeah," I say. "When's the appointment?"

"Five," she says, checking her phone. "Local time. See you there?"

"Yeah."

"I made you an appointment, too."

"Awesome," I say. "Sounds like fun."

"I hope so. If you don't show, I'll have to listen to Bethany blather about her roots for two hours."

She snorts as she stands up and stalks off, looking for her brother.

I leap to my feet and run off to find him first. On the

way, I pass Jordan and Flavortown...Trevor. They watch me pass, side-eyed, like conspirators.

It's paranoia, that's all it is. I've known Alex for two years. He's a great guy. I could totally see those two getting a hand job in a strip club, but not Karen's husband to be. Not a chance.

If I keep repeating that, eventually I might stop feeling all paranoid about it.

Okay, if I was a Colton, where would I be? This is a teeny little island, it can't be that hard to find him, right?

"He can't have gotten far," I say.

It's too bad I can't just follow Karen. Makes sense his sister would know where he'd be. Doesn't it?

First, I head to the beach. It's not a long walk. This, after all, is an island. Then it hits me. A bar, maybe? He likes to drink. No, that's silly, it's nine in the morning. I end up wandering, looking around and fighting the temptation to call his name.

Everything here is awash with color. It almost hurts my eyes, especially with the too-bright sun. I wish I could relax, but what Karen said is really bothering me. That, and it's been over an hour since I've seen Colton and I'm desperate to find him and...I don't know.

I find him sitting in a park by himself, in the shade of a tree. Perched on a picnic table, he sits with his chin propped on his hand like a statue and doesn't stir as I walk up beside him. Slowly edging around to where he can see me, I bend to the side.

"What?"

"We need to talk," I say.

He looks over at me.

"I hate that phrase."

"Listen," I say. "Karen said something really weird at breakfast."

"She's got cold feet, right? Don't worry about it. She wouldn't have planned all this if she didn't want to go through with it. She's too tenacious to let anyone buffalo her into a lifetime commitment."

"Is she?" I say. "It's not that. It is that, but she said something weird. She asked me how things went at the bachelor party."

He looks at me, alarmed.

"I don't mean that," I say quickly. "I mean, she thought we were going to an arcade and then going gambling. She didn't know about the strip club."

He laughs. "Is that what this is about? What did you think, Trevor and Jordan were going to tell her where they were taking us? There's such a thing as an open secret."

I hop up on the table and sit next to him.

"Not from me. I lied, Colt. I told her we went to an arcade."

He offers a hand. "Welcome to the secret fraternity of manhood."

I stare at it, unamused. "Right. No."

He waves me off. "You're her best friend. Sometimes best friends have to tell little white lies."

"She told me to stay away from you, too," I tease. "Basically called you a man slut."

"That's not the worst thing she's called me."

"What is it with you two?"

He looks down at his foot, watching the toe of his shoe bob as he digs his heel into the old silvered wood of the bench.

"I think it comes down to how our parents treated us. Karen was sort of an afterthought. I don't think she was really planned. Or at least, they didn't plan on a girl. My mom couldn't have more kids after her. My dad doesn't know what to do with her. Mom raised her, and Mom is…"

"She's told me," I say.

"Yeah. I don't know. Sometimes I feel like I should be closer with her. I don't have many other people in my life. Just work, travel. I don't like staying anywhere very long. What about you? You have any sisters?"

"We're not close," I say. "Just the one. My sister is fraternal twins with one of my brothers."

"How many of you all together?"

"Six of us," I say. "One girl, five boys."

"Shit," I say.

"Just my mom, too. Dad died when I was eight, I don't really remember him that well anyway. He wasn't around much. We lived in this old farmhouse outside Philadelphia. There used to be an actual farm, but my grandfather was a drunk and a gambler and sold it all off except for the house. They built a subdivision around it."

"Yeesh," he says. "Must not have been a lot of room."

"Yeah," I sigh. "Three bedrooms. Once Larissa, my sister, got older, she had to share my mom's room and the rest of us split the other two. It was all we could do to keep the lights on. I got a job as soon as I could get a working age waiver, like when I was fourteen. We all did. Even my youngest brother worked under the table when he was twelve."

"What happened?"

"She passed away. The house was delinquent on property taxes and we couldn't afford to keep it, so we sold it. There was a little bit for each of us after the taxes were paid, so we all took our cuts and went our separate ways. Except my oldest brother. He was already in the Marines and just sent a letter back saying to split his share between the other five."

"Damn," he says. "That had to be rough."

"Yeah. Lucky for me I got a scholarship and met your sister. I've gotten a lot of work through her. It's hard to be totally on your own at our age, you know? Hard to find work, steady pay in a place where I can feel safe."

"Feel safe?"

"Look at me, man. I'm not exactly Captain America over here."

He snorts. "I guess. How long have you been...you?"

I laugh. "It doesn't work like that, dude. I didn't turn you gay. We're not vampires. I am what I am, always have been, always will be."

"I wish I was that confident."

"Dude, you land airplanes on ships. How the hell are you not that confident?"

He clears his throat.

"It's not a big deal. I don't like talking about it."

His expression darkens.

"Did something happen?"

"Yeah. A war."

I blink a few times. "Okay. I won't push."

"What are you doing today?" he says, guarded.

"I have to be at the hairdresser at five. Moral support for Karen. Unless you want to go, too."

He quirks his brow.

"Yeah, I figured," I say, sighing. "Well, it'll be fun for me. We get our hair did together all the time."

"I don't understand you," he says.

"Are we going to sit here all day or what? There must be something to do on this island."

"Yeah."

"Something really is bugging me," I say, as he stands up. "I didn't watch Alex as close as I should have. He did go into that wine spritzer room or whatever it is alone with those girls."

"You know, half the point of a strip club scene like that is to embarrass the guy. I'm sure he's been around the block a few times, and Karen has, too."

"I know, but it's really nagging at me. They were doing that when Karen and her friends were off playing laser tag."

Colton frowns. "Why didn't we get to play laser tag?"

"I know," I huff.

"Look," he says. "If you want to get the real truth on what happened, we could go find Flavortown and slap him up a bit."

I flinch. "Really? What would that accomplish?"

"It would accomplish me getting to smack him up a bit. Which is something I'd like to do very much."

I laugh. "No slapping Trevor, Colton. Karen is worried you won't behave."

I walk with him up the street. He seems cagey, eyes snapping everywhere. Naturally, I start to follow all those looks. There doesn't seem to be anything threatening here. The whole place just oozes quaintness.

Colton doesn't shoo me away, at least. He walks next to me down the street. We're not the only ones out, of course. The place is riddled with vacationers. The more people are around, the more nervous he seems to become.

"What's bugging you?" I ask him.

He clears his throat. "Just worried we'll be seen."

"You know," I say, "If anyone sees you with me, they won't immediately jump to conclusions."

He frowns slightly. "Some people will. My father. Last thing I want is him starting something at the wedding. I just want Karen to get through this and have a good time."

I nod appreciatively. "I get that, but she's not really

having a good time. She really does seem nervous about Alex."

"I told you, the strip club thing is nothing," he says. "Nothing happened. Nothing he hasn't seen before. Unless he makes a habit of it, it's water under the bridge."

Despite that, after a few more minutes of walking, he glances at me and says, "What do you know about him?"

"Alex?" I say. "Why?"

"I barely know the guy. Karen doesn't keep in touch like she did when we were younger. She's too busy with her work and all that, and I can be hard to reach."

"What exactly is it that you do, anyway?"

"I asked about Alex."

"Well," I say, "they met at a meetup. Karen needed connections—friends and stuff, but also business people. She went to meetups for young entrepreneurs. They met there. Alex had a little online marketing outfit he was running."

"Marketing what?"

I shrug. "Whatever made ends meet. Homeopathy, ghostwritten self-help books, herbal remedies."

Colton stops. "Karen is marrying a scam artist?"

I shrug. "The gig economy is like that, Colt. People do what they have to do. I have a little sideline I don't tell anybody about, besides all the freelancing I do and work for Karen."

He eyes me. "Like what?"

"Nothing," I say. "I haven't told her. Why would I tell you?"

"I could make you tell me," he says smoothly.

"Is that a threat?"

"Maybe it's a promise."

I shudder all over. I was barely paying attention to where we were walking. We've just sort of arrived at the beach without really planning on getting there. The sand is gleaming bleached white, so bright I have to shade my eyes while Colton squints, leaning on a wooden rail. The boardwalk along the beach is lined with curious wooden benches. The backs swing forward and back, so you can sit facing either the water or the land. An empty bandstand dominates the scenery, draped in flags that catch the cool breeze off the ocean.

Despite the breeze, I'm hot. Colton is sweating. He pulls up his shirt to swipe his face dry, baring his incredibly muscular stomach and thick bands of muscle that ridge down to his hips. When he drops the shirt, he catches me staring and our eyes lock.

I start walking, almost daring him to follow. Looking around, I look for a likely spot, my heart pounding in my chest. The beach is covered with people and a riot of colorful blankets and umbrellas.

There's an alleyway between two buildings, in the shade. I duck out of view and my pulse pounds even harder as I sense Colton approaching behind me. His presence is like a subtle pressure on my back, like there's too much of him and he escapes himself. As soon as we're out of view I grab his belt buckle and lick my lips.

He leans back against the wall. I pull his shirt up and press my lips to his stomach. The coarse hair tickles my chin as I work down, gliding my tongue along the ridges and valleys of his muscles. His breathing quickens with barely contained power and his hands settle on my shoulders, a gentle pressure moving me onto my knees.

I undo Colton's belt as I work my mouth down his body and press my lips to the base of his cock. I draw his pants down more and more, running my lips down his shaft as he stiffens against me. He lets out a soft moan as I reach the tip and draw it into my mouth. The thickness swells between my lips, and he takes my head in his hand, pushing roughly.

I dig my fingers into his ass and press down, driving him deeper into my mouth, sucking hard and rolling my tongue as I stare up at him. He clenches his teeth and relaxes against the wall, still holding my head as I work him with my lips and tongue.

He keeps glancing towards the alley entrance.

"Someone might see us," he says, very softly.

My world contracts and closes in around us as I focus on him. He jerks when I cup his balls in my hand, running the other up his stomach. The muscles clench and heave as pleasure ripples through his body. My own cock tightens in my shorts, a dull pleasant weight between my legs.

He grows harder and harder with each stroke of my lips, each flick of my tongue. I let him slide from my mouth and run my lips up the underside of his shaft.

"Fuck," he mutters. "Careful. I'll blow all over your face."

"Fuck my throat," I purr, surprised at myself.

I usually don't like it so rough, but something about him twists open a valve inside me. There's a hollow that needs to be filled, and the excitement, the rush of when he cuts loose on me, is like a drug.

He doesn't argue. He doesn't apologize. He grabs my head, fingers in my hair, and thrusts. I can barely breathe, choking with gagging as his hard cock pushes too deep, thrust into me until his balls hit my chin, again and again, but the ecstasy of it rolls through me in cooling waves until I can feel my own dick grow impossibly hard and sticky with a bead of precum.

Colton grunts as he comes, holding my head in his hand as he pumps his seed down my throat. Even as he finishes and his muscles slacken, he pulls me to my feet and crushes me in a kiss. I want to fuck him now, have him inside me right here where anyone can walk up on us, but I don't dare.

He grabs my cock through my pants and squeezes. I yelp, too loud.

"I should do something about this."

My whole body is a single huge heart, clenching a pulsing rhythm. He massages me through my clothes.

"Stop," I whisper. "I don't want a big stain on my shorts."

He releases his hand from my crotch and pushes me into the wall, savaging me with hot, passionate kisses. He's like an unleashed animal, finally free of ancient bonds. It's all I can do to drag his pants up and do up his belt for him.

Finally, he releases me.

"I want you again," he says, his voice strained.

He rocks his hips, pumping himself against me. He's hard again, already, and his cock rubs against mine through my clothes. I let out a little purring sound and wrap my arms around him, my hands chasing up his back as he nibbles at my throat.

"I have to get to the hairdresser," I protest.

"Fuck the hairdresser," he snarls.

"I thought you wanted to fuck me."

He barks a laugh. "You know what I mean."

"Maybe later," I say. "Isn't there some macho ritual you're obligated to attend?"

"Yeah," he groans, annoyed. "As a matter of fact, there is."

CHAPTER 5

COLTON

I slip into my dinner jacket and out of my hotel room, reflecting that the linen, at least, keeps me somewhat cooler than wool would. I have my father to blame for this, and for the sweat-soaked dress shirt I'll be tossing in the laundry later. With the bachelor party dealt with, it's time for a more formal gathering.

He rented a room. He knows there's a no smoking policy, and he doesn't care, and the hotel staff don't care to correct him. The drawing room is an ornate relic of times when people occupied spaces called drawing rooms, all wood paneling, dark carpeting, and leather furniture. The smell of my father's cigar hits me like a wall. He smokes enormous Churchills that last for hours and stink up whatever space he occupies, the stink surrounding him like an aura.

He's not the only one smoking. My cousin Trevor delights in the absurdity of it all. He struts around the room holding an oversized cigar in one hand and a brandy snifter in the other, while clad in silk trousers and a peach colored smoking jacket. His sunglasses are still perched on his head.

Dad looks at him occasionally, the way he looks at staff he's trying to ignore. He's taken up residence in a massive throne of a wingback chair, with Alex seated next to him. There's an empty seat saved for me.

As soon as I sit down, a drink girl saunters over. Dad leers at the young woman, and I find myself noting that she's almost six years younger than Karen. He rather blatantly stares at her ass as she quietly asks me what I want.

"Cognac," I say, waving her off.

"Glad you could join us, Colton. I was just getting to know my new son-in-law. I think we should both be better acquainted with him. He's to be family."

Alex looks like he'd rather be anywhere else, and I can't blame him.

"I was wondering," Dad goes on in that tone he uses where he always presumes he has the most interesting thing to say in his immediate circle, "when you and Karen will be moving out of that city. No place to raise a child."

"Have you been there?" I ask before Alex can bumble through an answer.

My father gives me a frigid look. "I haven't had the pleasure."

You've never been west of Pennsylvania, I nearly point out to him, but catch myself.

"I've been there a few times. Lovely city. Karen lives in Ballard. Lovely neighborhood."

"So I'm told," Dad says. "A little too bohemian for my tastes."

Everything is too bohemian for his tastes.

"I was just asking Alex what it is that he does, again."

Dad's words roll off his tongue, adding to his insufferable air. He has a way of asking what an acquaintance does for a living with an air of arrogant reproach, as if they lose points for being pressured into working like a serf instead of choosing to be rich, like he is.

"I suppose I'd call myself a businessman," Alex explains. "I've been selling and marketing since I was sixteen."

Dad clears his throat. "So you're in sales, then. I've never grasped how one makes a career at that with all this on-line. In my day, sales was an honest living, even if it was a little lower class. Traveling hither and yon to sell boots and such from a sample case."

Alex looks at my father like he's an alien, and tight lines of annoyance form at the corners of his mouth. I feel a little jerk of annoyance at myself for having essentially the same reaction. At least I questioned what he was selling, instead of just being a generic dickhead like my father.

He's putting on airs, anyway. He's only fifty-four. Traveling salesmen my ass. His only knowledge of sales probably comes from the Arthur Miller play.

As insufferable as Dad is, I'm curious, too.

"What exactly is it you've been selling?" I ask.

"Oh, all sorts of things," Alex says, not a hint of nerves as he shifts in his seat. "I started off thrifting. Going to thrift shops and yard sales, that kind of thing, selling it on eBay. Physical goods are too much of a pain in the...too much of a hassle, though. You need space, have to cover shipping costs, have to cover inventory costs. I started drop shipping."

"May I ask what that is?" Dad asks, drolly.

"I marketed stuff and had it shipped straight to the customer from the manufacturer."

"Isn't that sales?" Dad says.

I clear my throat. "Sounds interesting. You've been doing that ever since?"

"Yeah. I expanded my product lines. Started selling eBooks, too. That's how I met Karen. We ran into each other at a meetup. When she told me about her business, I was all over it, but our relationship couldn't stay professional."

My eyes narrow. Something is off. The waitress hands me my drink and I swirl it before taking a gulp. The heat drops down into my chest like boiling water dumped on ice, oddly welcome.

"I'm not sure about my daughter marrying a salesman," Dad says.

I'm torn between my grating annoyance at him and my unease about Alex. What Julian told me has been boring into the back of my thoughts all afternoon, a constant itch that's too deep to scratch.

Alex, for his part, is pretty taken aback. He's probably never met anyone like my father, which is like meeting a cross between the guy in the Monopoly logo and an annoying uncle who doesn't quite say anything worth flipping the Thanksgiving table over, but constantly tows the line.

"I have a lot in common with Karen. We both built ourselves up from scratch."

Karen, if she were here, would debate that. She definitely had financial support from the family. She told me they were covering her rent when she moved out to Seattle and had to talk them out of buying her a house. She's always been humble, much to the annoyance of my father.

"Yes, she did," he says immediately. "It's quite impressive how she's built herself up from nothing, even if she's sunk all her time into building a business selling face paints to children and housewives to make themselves look like clowns. I swear, half the kids today look like they belong in the circus, and the other half like they belong in prison."

It's only the structural integrity of the shape of a brandy snifter that keeps it from shattering in my grip. Alex's beet-red face and staring eyes tell me he's thinking of throwing his drink in Dad's face.

"If you two ever want real work, you can always come back East and I'll find you some worthwhile positions under me. Karen isn't fit to run the company, of course, that's for Colton."

If Karen were here she'd snap at him that she is doing a real job and he's never worked a day in his life. I'm tempted to share the message in her honor, but I don't want to cause a spectacle on the night before her wedding.

When I say spectacle, I mean a brawl that spills out onto the beach and turns into a riot.

"I think we'll be fine," Alex says, eyeing me for a moment. "Karen is going to expand her business."

"That's all well and good," Dad says, dismissively.

Alex and I both sit there and stare at him for a moment, waiting on him to continue. Usually when people say, "that's all well and good," they say, "but," and complete their thoughts. Dad says it the way people say, "bless your heart." Alex isn't prepared for it.

I rise. "Alex, why don't we take a walk?"

"I could use some air," Alex says, casting a glance at my father.

"Don't dawdle," he says. "I have more to ask."

As I step away, Trevor takes my seat next to him. The look on Dad's face is worth enduring Flavortown's questionable taste in clothes, food, and existence.

I open the door and step out onto the porch with Alex. The sea breeze coming off the water is cool at night, and refreshing. My clothes will stink of Dad's stogie until I've washed them. Alex sniffs at his own lapel.

"It's permanent," I say. "Have to dry clean to get it out."

He clears his throat. "The old man asks a lot of questions."

"I'm not going to tattle if you tell me he's a dick."

Alex cracks a smile.

"I do feel like I need to get to know you," I say, leaning back against the railing. "You are marrying my sister in the morning."

He looks into his drink the way people do when they're trying to conceal an expression. I watch him intently.

"I should get to know you. See what kind of family I'm marrying into."

"I wouldn't worry about that. Karen isn't dragging you to any Thanksgiving dinners, I expect."

"He ask you about the bachelor party?"

Alex shoots me a look. "No."

"He probably won't," I say, turning to look out into the water. "It wouldn't be gentlemanly. Sometimes it's like he thinks he owns a plantation, or he's one of those guys that hung out in an explorer's club in London with a bunch of stuffed elephants."

Alex relaxes visibly.

"I am, though," I add.

He looks over at me. "You were there."

"I wasn't with you the whole time. Anything happen in that private room that I need to know about?"

Alex turns, facing me. "Why are you so curious all of a sudden? When we were out, you had a stick up your ass the whole time, and you snuck off the first chance you got and went to get trashed."

I straighten, swirling my snifter of cognac, one hand tucked behind my back.

"Man to man," I say. "If anything happened, this is your chance to come clean before the deed is done. You say no, I'll believe you."

He stares me straight in the eye. "No."

"I believe you," I say.

Do I believe him? I'm not sure.

"Good," he says. "Glad we got it out in the open. You coming back inside?"

"In a few," I say to dismiss him.

Once I'm alone, I down the rest of my drink and set the glass on the railing. Something is bothering me about him. I didn't pay Karen's beau much mind during our week in Vegas. I spent most of it avoiding him. Now, we're on a tiny little island and the proximity is bringing things into focus.

There is bad blood between me and Karen. The last time we really talked, we parted on bad terms, and yet we've kept in passive-aggressive touch.

Leaning on the railing, I watch the waves roll in as the sun sets. It really is beautiful here, a perfect place for a wedding. The hotel staff are putting everything up for that now, building a trellis for the ceremony in the morning.

I never really knew what, specifically, set Karen off and prompted our argument. I only know that she's had it in for me ever since, and over time, as she grew from a bratty sister into an annoying adult, I had less and less tolerance for her snippy attitude and dialed-back contact during the holidays.

Even though she's been icy to me since I arrived back in Vegas, she was weirdly strident in her invitation to her wedding. Almost pleading with me in the voicemail she left after I didn't RSVP fast enough.

Something about this whole situation is bothering me. It's like trying to read a page from a book, but it's so close to my nose, I can only see a few blurred words.

I step inside just in time to hear my father mutter, "What the hell?"

Julian has arrived. I don't think anyone thought to invite him, but he must have found his way here by the inertia of all the men gathering in one place. Either that, or Karen sent him to spy again. He walks into the room wearing a dress shirt and slacks as awkwardly as a kid.

For too long, I stare at him. The hairdresser trimmed and...shaped his hair, I don't have a word for it, but it sits somewhere between a slightly long haircut for a man and a feminine bob. They also frosted the tips with dye or bleach or something so there's a mix of light gray and iridescent green, almost like snow in his hair.

My father glares contemptuously at him as he shuffles toward a corner to hide.

"I can't believe my daughter is forcing us to endure that creature in the wedding party," my father says in the shout-whisper of someone who only cares to pretend he isn't being heard.

"What did you call him?"

The words escape my mouth before I can even think. The sound seems to ping off all the glasses and decanters in the room, and the cocktail waitresses look up from what they were doing, not watching.

Dad turns slowly, like a mummy in a cheesy old horror movie. He looks advanced beyond his years, dry and desiccated like Boris Karloff in a smoking jacket. He's spent his whole life trying to look old and dignified and only managed half of that.

"Pardon me?"

"I said, what did you call him?"

"I'm afraid I don't quite know what you mean," he says.

"Don't bullshit me," I snap, my voice cracking around the room.

Trevor slinks away. Across the room, Alex looks over, jaw set tight as his fingers go white around his whiskey glass.

"It doesn't matter," Julian says, turning to leave.

"You wait right there," I say, thrusting out a finger. He freezes in place as though I'd thumped his chest, even though he's ten feet away. "I want the old man to tell me what he said."

"I'm afraid I don't quite know what you mean," Dad says smoothly. He starts to turn away from me.

I take a bounding step towards him. Trevor grabs my arm.

"Hey, man," he says nervously. "Maybe you've had a little too much to drink."

He's trying to offer me a chance to save face and back down from my father. Fuck that and fuck him.

"I'm sick of your goddamn imperious attitude," I tell the old man. "Fucking look at me when I talk to you."

"Son," he says, "You've clearly had a little bit too much to drink. Why don't you go take a breather?"

"No. The country club bullshit is over, you obnoxious old prick. I'm sick of you acting like you're king of the universe because of my grandfather's money. You sit there on your privileged ass and judge people and spew your bullshit and we all have to sit here and take it? Fuck that and fuck you."

He launches to his feet. "Boy, don't you——"

"What? Huh?" I snap. "Let's see what you got, old man. You think playing polo got you ready to tangle with me?"

Julian stares at me, imploring.

Dad stares me down. Or rather, up. I've got a good three inches in height on him.

"This isn't the time or the place," he says. "We're here for your sister's wedding. Don't embarrass her."

"Like you give a goddamn," I say, turning on my heels.

I storm out of the drawing room and down the hall, and then outside. It's still light out, and too hot to wear a damned jacket. I rip it off and throw it in the sand as I walk out onto the beach and plop down on my ass. A wave rolls up around me, soaking my slacks and thousand-dollar dress shoes. I don't give a damn, I have more.

The water, cold as it soaks through to my rump, makes me shiver. My shivers turn into a gale of laughter, echoing into the dark night.

Footsteps behind me. Julian walks down the sand, holding his shoes and socks in his hand.

"Hey."

"Hey," I say, hoarsely.

"You're ruining your shoes."

"So what?" I say.

"They're nice shoes."

"I can buy more," I say. "That's all it's good for. Buying shoes."

"Look," he sighs, sitting next to me. "I don't want you to think I'm not grateful. Leaping to my defense like that was really great of you. Also kinda hot. Also, a little romantic. I'm just worried you didn't think it through."

"Did you hear what he said?"

"Yeah, I did," Julian says. "You really think my skin is that thin?"

"That isn't the point," I say. "That old shitbird has lived his life doing and saying whatever he wants, and nobody has ever taken him down a peg."

"Did you take him down a peg?"

I huff. "Probably not. He just won't care."

"I thought you wanted to keep things quiet," he says.

"Yeah. You shouldn't be here. Go back to the hotel."

"I'm not leaving you alone."

I let out a long sigh.

"Is there a lot of bad blood between you two?"

I glance his way, and then out at the ocean. "About that much," I say, flicking my hand towards it.

"What happened?"

"My life happened."

Julian is quiet for a while. Waiting.

"My whole life has been built around carrying on his legacy," I explain. "Before I put my foot down, he was pushing me towards politics. The whole military career was supposed to set me up for a run at a Congressional seat. He tried to make me get married."

"What does that mean?" Julian says. "Make you how?"

I clear my throat. "Pressure. Constant, overwhelming pressure. That's why I went on my world tour, I guess you could call it. I couldn't set foot in my own home without being hounded and badgered, and…"

I can't finish the thought, because it's a lie. That's not the reason I've been avoiding my father, why I resent him so much. Why I resent myself. I keep staring at my hands. Wet sand has worked into the creases in my palms and knuckles somehow. I don't remember putting my hand down, but I must have.

"Somebody might see us," Julian says. "I'm going back to my room. I'll leave the patio door open."

He rises, giving me a longing, curious glance before he heads up the beach. I sit there for a while longer as the waves roll further up the sand behind me. Finally, I get up, and, soaked, start up the beach.

Karen is waiting for me in the dune grass.

"What the hell happened? Everyone is talking about it."

"I blew up at the old man," I say, starting past her.

She catches my arm in her hand and tugs. "I need more than that."

"I'm not going to make a scene at your wedding."

"I don't care about that. I need to know what's going on. Don't leave me out of the loop."

"Dad got into some of his usual bullshit and I got in his face over it. That's all."

"In front of my fiancé," she says.

"Yeah. Look, he said something terrible about your friend and I couldn't let it go."

"Were you drunk?"

"I hadn't had anything in hours," I say. "Just one drink. Cognac."

"Hard stuff," she says.

"I'm not a goddamn alcoholic," I snap.

She releases my arm.

"I don't know whether to thank you or slap you. You found a way to do what I want and piss me off at the same time."

"Yeah. I'm like that," I grumble.

"You're different," she says. "Something is off. You're not acting like you used to. You were obnoxious and a brat."

"Funny, I thought the same thing about you."

She sneers at me. "Cute. Are you going to talk to me or not?"

"No," I say, shaking loose.

"Fine," she sighs. "Just don't start anything at the wedding. Or the reception. Avoid Dad if you have to, and please don't drink too much."

"Why are you talking to me like I have a drinking problem?"

"I don't know. I'm a little worried, Colton. There's something really dark going on in that head of yours and you're not telling anyone what it is."

"I'm fine," I say. "I just got older. You don't act like you used to, either. You're still an annoying little prat, but you're so…adult , now."

"Oh, thanks," she says. "I really appreciate it."

"You don't deserve the shit Dad gave you all your life."

"Thanks," she says, folding her arms. "It'd have been nice if you'd said something when it was actually happening."

"Yeah," I say. "It would have. If you'll excuse me."

I leave her in the grass, sick to my stomach. I didn't even think to say anything about her husband. How could I? Julian is probably just being paranoid and protective of his friend, and if I raised the issue, she'd probably take it as if I were trying to put a damper on her big day.

Karen is a big girl. She's been dating this guy for over a year. I'm sure she's ready. It's hard not to look at her and see my little sister anymore—my bratty, demanding, pushy little sister. Not that I blame her. It was the only way she got attention from our parents. I don't think they noticed she existed until I was out of the house.

On my way back to my room, I stop and remember what Julian said. Taking the long way around, I approach the patio doors, counting down until I find his. Unlocked, just as he said it would be. It slides freely and a rush of cool air meets my face as I slip inside, carrying sweet, waxy scents.

He lit candles.

Carefully, I close the door.

"Are you here?" I say.

"I'm here," he says, stirring on the bed. Reclining on the pillows, he has a book resting on his chest and small glasses perched on the tip of his nose. Rather than make him look older, they give him the appearance of trying to look older, like a newbie librarian trying to fit in with aged peers. He slips them off and extends his leg.

He's naked, the flickering lights from the candles playing across his pale skin. Lying on his back, it's easy for me to see his breath quicken as I approach. His cock, fully hard, lays against his stomach, rising and falling with it and pulsing with the beat of his heart. He's left a box of condoms and a bottle of lube on the bed.

"You have me at a disadvantage," he says.

I fumble for the buttons on my shirt. Julian slips off the bed and pads over to me. Just the sight of his erection quivering in front of him as he moves brings me to full hardness. He rises on the balls of his feet and plants a kiss on my lips as his fingers deftly work the buttons, his hands moving lightly over my chest as he bares it to the cool air.

I slip out of that and he undoes my belt, slipping his hand under my cock as he pulls my underwear down. He lifts me out of my clothes with a kind of reverence, holding my shaft in his hand, then in both, stroking it. He looks up at me with a purse-lipped smirk and cups his hand around the head of my cock while he strokes the shaft lightly in his hand.

My entire body tightens. I reach for him and he slips away, darting for the bed. The sight of him moving in the nude fills me with a heady, almost drunken feeling. I shed the last of my clothes and follow him. He lies on the bed face down, spread eagled, with his cock pressed under him, jutting between his legs. I skim my hands down his back and crawl on top of him, pushing him into the yielding mattress with my weight.

His entire form pulses under me. His skin, so pale, is warm just on the surface but hot underneath and the scent of him fills my nostrils when I breathe in, my face pressed into his hair. He undulates under me, his ass rising into a position of presentation. So submissive, so eager.

Julian twists out from under me onto his back. I roll on top of him and we start to wrestle, skin on skin, naked bodies intertwined. I pin him and steal a kiss, let him wriggle loose, pull him to me. The look on his face screams excitement when I display strength, when I grab him by the hips and pull him to me. I wrap my mouth around his cock and suck. He groans, shivering, fingers gliding over my scalp.

He actually pushes me away when he starts to get close, then rolls over and presents himself to me. I toy with his balls, watching the look on his lovely face as my finger traces around his ass. When I make it slippery with lube, it slides inside him and his face goes slack. I pump my finger in and out while I slide a condom down my cock, working a second one in as I pump in my fist, opening him up. I can't wait to feel his hot, quivering body tighten and pulse around me.

Moving on top of him, I press my chest into his back, arching to guide the tip of my cock, now slick with lubricant, into his ass. He gasps as I enter him, moaning and driving his chest into the bed to raise his ass and take me faster. As I enter him, I push him down, driving in deep until he starts to shake, a wordless sound caught between his clenching teeth. When I draw back and thrust again he lets a little *ahh*, a short noise that melts into a moan, a little high pitched.

The cries coming from him make me slow, wondering if he's in pain, until he whispers "harder, do it harder," and I do, throwing my weight into it. His hands ball into fists and he bites his lip so hard it turns the skin white, his eyes pressed tightly shut. He clenches around me, squeezing my cock so I can barely move. I reach under me and add more lube so I can move faster, and Julian shudders and shivers, his toes squirming on the bed.

Slowly I glide out of him and roll onto my back. He seems confused for a moment before he crawls on top of me and lowers himself onto my cock. I watch myself enter him with hunger, savoring the sensation of his body forced open by my girth as he takes me. Back arched, he rests his hands on my stomach and rolls his hips, using me as an instrument of pleasure as I come closer to exploding. His cock bobs above my stomach, his balls tight and hard and ready.

I grab his hips and control his motions. I'm so ready to come, it almost hurts, pain tightening in little muscles in my stomach as I hold back. Looking at him, shining with sweat, he's so...beautiful. Never a word I thought I'd choose to describe a man, but there it is. Julian is gorgeous, a work of art. For a moment that seems to stretch on, I watch him undulate and shudder as he rides me, consuming the way his lithe, elegant swimmer's body moves.

He arches back and cries out. Without a single touch, his cock pulses and he comes, his body shaking all over as he orgasms on top of me. The clenching of his body is what drives me over the edge and I thrust into him from below, hard and fast, heedless, clasping his wrists to pull him down onto my cock as I hammer it into him like a battering ram while the orgasm is still taking him. I come, and grunt, then moan, louder and longer than I ever have before.

He slumps forward, hands on my chest, panting, stomach twitching in and out as he breathes.

"Holy shit," he whispers.

"Yeah," I pant, "Damn."

He groans when he draws away, sliding me out of his body. He flops down on his bed and lies there, then rolls off, stumbling into the bathroom. I follow a moment later when I hear the shower running.

He's standing in the spray in the glass cabinet, lathering himself with soap. I push inside with him and pin him to the wall.

Julian is wearing a shower cap.

"Don't want to mess it up," he says.

I roll my eyes. "Right."

"I need to actually, like, take a shower."

He says that, but he doesn't protest.

"What if I want more?"

"Do you want me to be limping tomorrow? I feel like I just got fucked by a bulldozer."

I run my hands up his sides and he rests his arms on my shoulders, looking up at me with his big eyes and pouty lips.

"Tomorrow is the big day. My sister is getting married."

"Yeah. I haven't talked to her since I saw her at the hairdresser."

"She talked to me after you left the beach."

I can see him tense.

"She can't know about us," he says.

"Why not?"

"She'll freak out. I don't know who she'll be mad at, but she'll be mad."

"Makes me wonder why you stay friends with her," I say.

Julian clears his throat and lets out a breath. "Karen treated me like a person, not a curiosity. I'm closer with her than I am with my own family. She's kind and caring. I know she can be snappy, but she's stressed out. She hasn't been the same for a few weeks."

He looks like he's holding something back from me. Not telling me something.

He slips past me and scours the soap from his skin under the spray. I appreciatively watch him step out of the shower and walk across the room to grab a towel. Soon after, I follow.

"Did you talk to Trevor?"

"You saw how that ended," I say wryly.

He huffs. "We have a wedding to attend, tomorrow." He gives me a sly look. "That's usually a big moment for couples."

I flinch. Couples. Julian stalks out of the shower, pulling me along with him.

He throws a towel on the bed and sits on it, shimmering with beaded water on his pale skin, his hair plaited against his neck. He scratches at the light stubble on his cheek and taps his feet.

"I need to know if I should say something," he says. "This is pretty much the last chance. We could go to Karen together and tell her what happened."

"We don't know what happened," I point out. "I talked to Alex. He seems alright to me. You'd think he'd set me off, if there was something wrong. He is marrying my sister."

"Who doesn't like you very much," Julian points out.

"It's more complicated than that," I say. "It's a long story."

"Tell me."

CHAPTER 6

JULIAN

I kick my feet, swinging my heels just above the carpet. Colton moves languidly as he rises to dress, tugging on the clothes he wore in here.

"When we were growing up, my father was obsessed with this idea of an heir," he explains. "You know we're fourth generation?"

"Immigrants?"

"Rich," he sighs. "My father would be happy to tell you, at length, about how his first ancestor in America stepped off the boat in sixteen-something something, like that makes him better than you. That's all he lives for, the things that make him better than you. Has a chip on his shoulder the size of a mountain."

"What did that mean for your sister?"

"It meant that to him, she's useless. She can't carry on the family name."

I blink a few times. "She is, though. She's not taking Alex's last name."

"I already heard all about that," Colton says, dropping into a side chair near the bed. "It's unseemly, according to him. Who uses the word 'unseemly' these days? I mean, really."

"There's been a competition thing between me and her since she was old enough to talk. She had to do everything I do, but better. I think if she could join the Marines and fly a jet, she would have. She probably would be better than I am, too. I've spent my whole life falling up. She actually made something of all her advantages."

"Falling up?" I say. Standing to dress.

I can feel Colton's eyes on my skin as I move. I make sure to bend at the waist in front of him and thrust out my ass as I pull my jeans up and do a little hop to seat myself properly in them before I sit down, shirtless.

"Everything was easy for me," Colton explains. "I never knew if I was succeeding because I was actually good at anything or because my father was donating buildings to my schools. How do you know if you're earning your grades when your teacher calls you 'sir'?"

"I couldn't relate," I say.

"That's why I went into aviation. I wanted to do something legitimately challenging and know that I was actually accomplishing something myself. I wanted a sense of meaning."

I nod slowly. "That I do understand."

He slumps in the seat. "Dad was livid when he found out. I was supposed to be a staff officer, you know? Only pilot a desk. The whole military career thing was supposed to be a resume point for when I run for office."

I frown. "You don't sound very enthusiastic for that."

"You know why I've spent the last couple years circling the world partying, being an idiot the whole time?"

"You never got the chance when you were younger?"

"Bullshit," he scoffs, "I was the same in college. No, I wanted to make sure there were plenty of pics of me in Dubai with floozies on my lap. Thank God for social media. Killed my political aspirations, that did."

"Why didn't you just refuse?" I say. "It's not like your father can make you run for office or whatever."

He leans forward, resting his hands on his thighs. "He controls the purse strings."

"Does he? You could do whatever you want. Look at Karen. She's got a whole empire going."

Colton smiles sadly. "Can I? I have no real skills and no experience."

"You could fly planes," I point out. "Jesus, you could be an airline pilot, even, if you had to."

"I guess," he says. "My real passion was always motorcycles. Not like the Harley thing, you know? English bikes. My grandfather had this fantastic Triumph Bonneville, absolutely beautiful. He left it to the family like everything else."

"Do you have it?"

Colton shakes his head. "I stole it when I was fifteen, took it out for a ride. Dad auctioned it off after that. He didn't want me putting myself in danger. Without me, the whole empire goes splat, you know?"

"That was a little dangerous," I say. "Right?"

"Yeah, I guess," he says. "As soon as I was away from home in college, I got a bike of my own. When your allowance is five figures, you can just go buy one."

My head spins at the thought. Just...*getting* all that money, as a college student.

"That's nuts," I say. "You seriously got that much every month?"

"Yeah," he sighs. "I sound like an entitled prick, don't I?"

"A little, yeah," I say, "but Mom always said money can't buy happiness."

Colton snorts. "Yeah, but if you gave her a bunch, would she have bought any sadness?"

I'm quiet for a moment. Colton clears his throat.

"That was an incredibly shitty thing to say. I'm sorry."

"Nah, it's alright," I say. "I didn't understand how poor we were when I was little, or even when I started working. It was just there, you know? It was my normal."

"I have no idea what that could be like," he says. "I never wanted for anything as a child. Everything I needed or wanted was just there."

"Then why do you sound so sad?" I ask.

"I don't know," he says.

I think he does, but I don't press. He stands and pulls on his shirt.

"I should go. We need our beauty rest. Big day tomorrow."

"Yeah," I say. "Big day."

He slips through the glass doors, pausing to look at me intently before leaving, as if committing the scene to memory. When he's gone, I pull the curtains and flop on the bed, exhausted and more than a little sore, but smiling.

Being with him feels so natural. I wonder if this is what Karen has with Alex when the pair of them are alone. Part of me wants to sneak over to Colton's room and knock on the glass and spend the night there, but if I do that, I can't get dressed in the morning.

Sighing, I lay out my clothes. The suit I'm to wear is all gauzy linen, light and airy to keep me from passing out in the heat. Despite that, the cut is formal, with a swallowtail coat appropriate for a morning wedding. I frown when I look at it, just for the color. I agreed to wear a peach colored suit to fit in with the peach colored bridesmaids' dresses, but now I'm regretting it with my complexion. I wish Karen had taken up my suggestion that we go blue.

"Bleh," I mutter.

Even though I need rest, I end up pacing, nervous. You'd think I was getting married tomorrow, for all I pad back and forth barefoot through the room thinking about...my husband.

I test the words in my mind, trying to make them real and not an accident of a drunken sham marriage that was probably a joke. We're legally united in the bonds of matrimony. Now, even after all the sex, it feels like a dream, something that didn't happen. If I don't focus on it, it'll float out of my mind and erode away to nothing, as dreams inevitably do.

I wish I knew what Colton was thinking about it, if he thinks about it at all.

It's stupid. It's absurd. It's childish. It's downright silly, but I feel like this was meant to happen. Greater things are grinding together, invisible gears under the floor of the world shifting us together like game pieces on a titan's game board. How could it feel any different? I've wanted him since I knew how to want, and now I've had him, and the need is not diminished at all. I don't know if it ever will be.

"I sound like a twelve-year-old," I mutter to myself as I prepare for bed.

When my head hits the pillow, sleep comes on so fast that it grabs me and pulls me under before I have time to think. Maybe it's jet lag, maybe it's all the exertion, maybe it's stress, but I'm out like a light.

The next thing I know, the light of dawn is slicing a razor beam across the room through the curtains. I rise, shower again, and take a razor to my face, carefully scouring my skin baby-smooth. Somehow I manage without cutting myself and go to get dressed.

Jacket over my arm, I head down to Karen's room.

When I knock, the door swings open.

"Karen?" I say.

Her bridesmaids, Bethany and the others, five in all, are already here. Beth is the only one she really knows that well, the rest are distant cousins. The youngest is fourteen. Normally I'm all about rocking my look, masculinity be damned, but I feel a little absurd in a matching suit to their dresses. Karen is seated, dressed in a breathtaking gown that's demure and sheer at the same time. She looks damn near angelic.

"You look incredible," I tell her.

"Thanks," she says, though her mood seems sour.

Last minute jitters. Cold feet. Has to be.

"You okay?" I ask.

"Just a little tired. Nervous. I can't get past..." she glances around.

"Yeah," I say, eyeing the others. We can't have a private conversation here.

"Are you ready?" I say. "We need to get you out, soon. Alex's best man should be here soon."

Karen nods and rises. She moves with such grace and poise, it surprises me. Ducking her head a little, she allows me to rest the crystal tiara and veil on her head and adjust them into place.

"It's hot in here and I can smell my own breath," she says.

The others don't seem amused, but she and I share a laugh.

The knock comes. Jordan is on time, in his swallowtail coat. Trevor is with him, and for once, he doesn't have his sunglasses perched on his head. He looks a little down, eyeing the floor, and it makes me nervous. Maybe he's just tired and strung out, or hung over. The drinking has pretty much gone on unabated since we got here, despite the genteel pretentiousness of Karen's parents.

"Everything is ready," Jordan says. "It's time."

Karen nods and the pair leave. Karen hesitates, giving them a head start so they can get into position outside. Her dress has no train, but I walk behind her anyway. We thread through the hotel and out to the beach. When Karen emerges into the blinding sunlight, a full brass band strikes up the wedding march, her head snaps up, and a rigid, straight-backed poise takes over her body like a foreign invader.

Following behind, smiling, I forget the awkwardness of my position in the wedding party as tears well up behind my eyes. I suck them back just as I catch sight of Colton, who's taken up position as one of the groomsmen, third in line after Trevor. The minister has a wind-chapped, deeply tanned face that reminds me of a sailor, like some fisherman clambered off his boat and put on vestments. Despite that, he's open and serene, grinning.

Karen takes her position and the rest of us file into place behind her. This is happening. The band's performance dies down, and the assembled crowd goes quiet.

"Dearly beloved," the minister begins, diving into a long soliloquy on the virtues of love and romance that I barely listen to.

I'm too busy staring at Colton. He eyes me from his place among the men, jaw set.

When the vows start, it catches me off guard. Karen arranged for a non-denominational ceremony, so there's little in the way of ritual or prayer, just some heartfelt words and then the whole thing gets started.

"Do you, Karen Steele, take this man…"

As he reads out the vows, I lock eyes with Colton, almost mouthing them with my lips pressed shut. His eyes narrow, and the tears welling up in my eyes aren't as much for Karen anymore. I want to stand where she's standing. I desperately want the fantasy to be real. Another day gone until I promised I'd annul the whole thing, but I can't. How can I?

My sniffles prompt chuckles from the crowd. Trevor glares at me.

The exchange of rings comes. Jordan fishes them from his pocket, and Alex slides the gold band around Karen's finger. She does the same, and it's done.

I wonder if she's thinking what I'm thinking. Actually, I know she is, because she's told me, loudly and at length. This is all a pretty big production for something that only actually takes about twenty minutes.

I guess at this point we'd be packing them off into a limo and the wedding party would be stuffing themselves inside to join the bride and groom, but we don't need to drive across the hotel grounds. More relaxed now, Karen walks out with her husband for the handshakes and, genuinely smiling, mingles with the guests for a moment.

The first thing she does when she gets a chance is rip the tiara off her head and discard the veil entirely, shaking her hair loose. The hairdresser did an amazing job; it falls around her shoulders in thick dark waves, like a waterfall of ink. My chest swells with a kind of affectionate jealousy.

Colton looks like he swallowed a live crawdad. He loosens his bow tie and shirt and starts towards me, only veering off at the last minute as if he realizes that he's not supposed to show any real interest in me.

Karen's father is eyeing me whenever he's not busy, watching me like he expects some kind of secret.

This whole thing is fifty times more tense than it has to

be and I'm starting to wonder when the explosion is going to come. Butterflies flit around in my stomach.

Karen in her radiance soaks up all the attention, so no one notices that weird little nonverbal exchange between me and Colton.

I hate this kind of thing. I feel like I'm just kind of here, moving with the wedding party. The schedule for the day arranged for a break between the wedding itself and the reception in the afternoon. The reception is casual, too; no stuffy clothes. I can't wait to get out of this suit— which, again, seems wasteful. My poor senses are tingling. It's ridiculous that someone paid for this outfit that I will wear once for an hour, even if it was Karen and she can afford it.

Karen and Alex lead one another off, formally breaking up the gathering.

When I get back to my room, I hear a knock at the glass doors. When I slide them open, Colton crashes into the room like a breaking wave, bowling me aside with his presence alone.

Being near him again is electric, like a tingling field surrounds his skin, reaching out to draw me in, like gravity. He's still in his suit.

Casually, flirtatiously, I shed my suit, putting a little bit of a striptease into it. Colton watches but doesn't seize the opportunity, even if he rises to the occasion—judging by that bulge.

Prancing around in my underwear, I select my outfit for the reception, laying it out from my suitcase.

Colton sits in my side chair, hands hanging from the arms, one foot out. Somehow it makes him look regal, like a statue of a roman general in meditative repose. He stares at the carpet as I tug on a pair of shorts.

"What's wrong?" I say.

He grunts.

"Come on, you didn't come in here for the chair."

I stalk over to him, and, after a moment's hesitation, lower myself into his lap, falling against his chest. His arm falls naturally around my waist, but he still seems to see through me, gaze locked on the middle distance.

Finally he says, without looking up, "I think I should have talked to her."

"Nothing happened," I say, jumping to my feet. "I was just being paranoid. It was just a manifestation of my own nerves or something."

"Nerves?" he says.

"This whole place puts me on edge. When I look around here, all I see is a bank balance rapidly declining."

"I thought Karen paid your way," he says.

"She did. I don't have to spend money myself for it to set me off. I just have to see other people spending it, you know?"

He frowns.

"I think it's a bad idea to dismiss your instincts like that. You should listen to them. Something being off like that might save your life. I need a drink."

"It's the middle of the day," I say.

Despite that, he slides me off his lap and rises, pulling out a bottle of hard stuff from the honor bar. He slugs it back and winces, sucking back a sharp breath through his teeth.

"Little hair of the dog," he says.

"You worry me a little with that."

He raises an eyebrow. "You've basically known me for eight days."

"Well," I say, crossing my arms, "I am your husband."

He winces.

"Partner," I say.

"That's better," he says, stepping closer. He slips his thumb along my chin. "If anybody here is the husband, it's me."

"It doesn't work like that," I say.

"Say we were to dance tonight," he says. "Who'd lead?"

"We could flip a coin. I don't know. Whoever feels natural. Probably you. I can't dance for shit."

I pull the bottle out of his hand and set it aside.

"I fucking hate weddings," he says, sinking into the chair again. This time, he holds his head in his hands. "You have no idea. No. Idea."

"Why? Bad experience at one?"

"Something like that," he mutters. "I'd rather not talk about that today."

"Right," I say. "Okay, I won't push. We really do need to get to know each other. Not just, you know, biblically."

"There's nothing biblical about what we do," he says, smirking at me.

Suddenly he's all swagger again, but it's exaggerated, fake.

"Alright," he says, glancing at his watch. "I'm going to go get dressed down to get lit up. See you at the fucking party."

He slips out through the door, leaving me frowning, curious. Something is really eating at him—this is the weirdest I've seen from him yet. He keeps swinging from something beyond his normal confidence, an absurd parody of himself, to these brief flashes of despair. I don't have to know him that intimately to know something is really, really eating at him. Ripping him up.

I pick a shirt and head to the party.

The reception is coming together on the beach. The hotel has put up raised platforms and decking so there's a dance floor. The cake is protected by a net tent, a monstrosity of icing and fondant as tall as a person. Karen is greeting wedding guests. She ditched her wedding gown for a long, flowing floral print dress obviously chosen for comfort. She now wears the tiara without the veil, the only concession to the whole bridal status thing.

Climbing the platform, I head for my spot. Since I'm on her side, so to speak, I end up sitting next to her mother and father. Thankfully, she sits between me and the old man, buffering us. The guests are filling in now. Servers are moving about, bustling as they get ready to lay out the wedding feast. Colton, though he was part of the groom's party earlier, sits beside me.

I tense as he sits down. He's dressed casually but he's so muscular he makes a drab polo and shorts look good. Leaning back casually into the sea breeze, he watches the middle distance again, sharp eyes on the lookout for something I can't even imagine. I wish I knew what was eating him up.

Karen leans back in her seat and talks quietly with Alex. Alex's best friend and best man Jordan fidget, toying with a set of index cards. He goes from shuffling them to reading them, mouthing the words. The toast, probably. Alex's parents aren't here, so his best man is stepping up to the toast role. Thank God that's traditionally from the groom's side. I doubt I'd enjoy Karen's dad musing about whatever until the food gets cold. The only thing that could make this party worse than giving him the spotlight is if a whale beached itself behind us while we all danced the Macarena.

If the Macarena starts playing, I'm out of here, I swear.

As the servers bring out the first course and distribute

small gifts, Jordan rises to stand, tapping a champagne flute with his fork.

"Marriage is the golden ring in a chain whose beginning is a glance and whose ending is eternity," he begins.

His toast ends up going very well, if only because he clearly sat down and strung together a list of wedding toast quotes that he Googled. Karen looks pleased.

Colton looks nervous. He's knocked back a full flute of champagne already and waggles his glass at one of the waiters for more. He's eyeing the bar, soon to be an open bar, too.

After the toast, it's time for dinner.

Karen chose the menu, and thankfully it's light. Her father eyes the arugula salad as if it personally offended him. Colton picks listlessly at his food, like a kid who's been denied permission to leave the dinner table. He all but leans his head on his hand.

Karen is talking to her husband. I don't want to talk to her mother. Colton is next to me.

I jab my elbow into his side. He shifts slightly and ignores me. I give him another poke.

"Stop that," he mutters very quietly.

"What's eating you?" I ask him softly.

"I don't like weddings," he mumbles, staring into his empty glass.

A waiter leans in and pours more. I almost try to stop him, but it's only champagne; Colton is a big man, and I'm sure he has plenty of tolerance. It's not my place. I'm his partner, not his mom.

If I am his partner. I still don't know if this is a fling or it's real. It feels real. I would feel like I'm in a magical land of enchantment if Colton wasn't acting like this was his sister's funeral and not her wedding.

I sit back as the plates are changed. The courses are

brief and the plates small, mostly seafood. I think everyone is eager to get up. Tradition dictates that Karen and Alex share a "first" dance, and the disc jockey is setting up on the stage nearby.

As the last of the plates are cleared away, the newly-weds rise and lead the way to the dance floor. Karen wields her bouquet like a torch, waving it around in the first real excitement I've seen from her all day.

As the women gather around, Jordan and Flavortown grab my arms and push me into the group with them. I glare at them, but by then it's too late. Karen turns her back and tosses the flowers.

I duck, hoping to hide behind one of her younger cousins and let them catch the bouquet. For a split second, I get a glimpse of the bridesmaids, annoyed at my pres-ence. The damn flowers seem to cascade through space, like an orbiting satellite. Ground control to Major Petunias.

Bethany body-checks me out of her way, trying to grab them for herself, but she miscalculates. Badly. Her hip-bop knocks me off balance and I take a halting twist-step and sputter in alarm as a wad of flowers crashes into my face. My arms snap up in instinct and boom, I'm holding the bouquet.

The entire wedding party and all the guests go silent, staring at me. The DJ just looks perplexed. Bethany gives me a shove.

"Do over," she blurts, giving me a push. "He doesn't—"

Karen cuts her off. "Yeah, he does. Hold them up, Julian."

Sheepishly, I lift the flowers overhead and step out of the crowd, desperate to get away and get rid of them before the death stares from the bridesmaids and female guests make me spontaneously combust. I stand next to Colton, holding the flowers.

He slowly looks my way, looks at them, and turns, clearing his throat.

Bethany is still complaining. "It's not fair, he—"

Karen gives her that patented death glare of hers, cutting off the objection. The disc jockey helps, ramping up some music so he can play off it and announce the other part of the ceremony, the garter.

Jordan and Trevor move to the center of the stage while Alex carries a chair to his bride. She stares at Colton and their eyes briefly lock. As if he were wading through hip-deep sand, Colton pushes into the crowd and does the same thing I did, trying to hide in the press.

Karen throws her foot up on the chair and hikes up her skirt. Her legs are bare but she's wearing the traditional garter anyway. As the cheers and jeers roll in, Alex slides the little band down her leg, twirls it around his finger, and tosses it.

It whips straight at Trevor.

Colton's arm snaps out as quick as a striking snake and he snatches the garter from the air moments before it lands on Trevor's head and holds it up. Trevor ducks, as if he was about to be hit. He probably felt the air from Colton's hand moving.

"Yo," Trevor blurts out in shock. "That was some Spider-Man shit."

Colton raises the garter high, then stuffs it down his pocket and heads straight for the bar. I turn towards him, but Karen has my arm.

"Come on," she shouts. "You promised."

With a heaving, desperate sigh, I hand off the bouquet and line up with Karen and Alex and most of the rest of the wedding party as...

Yeah, it's the fuckin' Macarena, and it's loud.

Their first dance is the Macarena. Oh, Karen.

"I'm not drunk enough for this," I shout.

Karen hip-checks me and I bump her back, laughing. The crushing tension in my chest starts to relent. After the song ends, and I am no longer awkwardly miming dance moves I can barely remember, I slip off to grab a drink from the bar while Karen and Alex have their real first dance, a slow one set to Elvis.

Watching them, the tension comes back into my chest. Karen seems legitimately at ease, more than that, they disappear into each other. It's like watching a projection of the couple on a screen. They are somehow separate from us, and ethereal.

Sighing, I lean against the bar and slug down a vodka and cranberry and motion for another. I need to loosen up.

Colton has gotten pretty damn loose already. He's actually smiling. Color me shocked.

I want to get him away from here, but if I disappear too soon, my absence will be noted. His would be, too. That would lead to a lot of awkward questions we can't answer.

Standing next to him, I whisper, "Dance with me."

"You know I can't," he says.

"I'll talk to Karen. Maybe if we're open with her, it'll start healing things between you."

Colton eyes me. "It's not her. It's my fucking father."

His voice is just loud enough to turn a few heads. I don't know if his dad heard; he's not in sight.

"Easy," I say. "How many have you had?"

"Not enough," he says. "Barkeep! More!" he bellows, slamming his glass down.

Trevor steps up to him. "Hey, man, maybe you should slow down."

"Maybe you should go eat a chicken fried steak," Colton snaps back.

Trevor stares at him, blinking a few times. "Huh?"

"Never mind," Colton snarls. "Get out of my face."

Trevor backs off, visibly annoyed. Still, he'd have some catching up to do at the bar before he dared start anything.

That doesn't make me feel any better. Colton is making me a little nervous.

Fuck it.

"Hey, why don't we get out of here," I say to him, very quietly.

"I can't ditch my sister's wedding," he says.

"Look at her," I say. "She's having the time of her life."

Colton looks over. Karen is picking bits of cake and icing off her cheeks. I suddenly realize I missed the cake mashing, and I'm a little miffed. I might as well not be here as it is. I'm half in and half out of the festivities.

"Stay a bit," he says, "then I'm leaving."

He leans over the bar and hunches above his drink, coveting it. He swirls the dregs, as if something I said gave him pause, and he doesn't drink. The bartender is watching him with one eye as he pours drinks for other guests.

I'm a little tipsy. I make my way back out onto the dance floor and gyrate a bit, circulating through the dancers. I dance with Karen a bit, but everybody seems to want a turn with the bride and groom. She has plenty of people paying attention to her. As much as I'd like to hang out with her, it's a welcome change. Back in Seattle, we often only have each other.

Still, I have a pang of sadness in my gut as I move away from her, back to the bar.

Colton is gone.

CHAPTER 7

COLTON

I hate walking on sand. Always have. Didn't do much of it when I was a kid. Beach trips were a rarity for my family. It was yachting instead. Dad went the whole nine yards, down to the boat shoes and white shorts, like some half-assed knock-off Kennedy off the Vineyard on his sailboat. He'd strut around in a captain's hat, but it was as absurd as a little kid on his dad's boat pretending to command imaginary gunnery crews against fantasy pirates.

Dad knew about as much about sailing as I know about flower arranging. The paid crew did all the work, and he rarely took the boat out into the open water, even though she was ocean rated and my Pops, what I called my grandfather, told me stories about the time he took her from Cape Hatteras all the way over to Ireland one summer.

The way I feel now is how I perceived him then. Hollow, ultimately meaningless, going through the motions for the sake of it and deluding himself into thinking he had mastered something he was only on the edge of. He wasn't a captain, he was a passenger. If you can't actually steer a boat, can you really be said to own it?

I can't steer my whole fucking life, how do I presume to own that?

Weddings. Goddamn weddings. Stumbling, I make my way along the beach, slipping and turning my ankles in the sand, nearly falling a few times. I abandoned my drink glass somewhere. I knocked back five neat scotch whiskeys too fast and now my head is stuffed full of pencil erasers, my balance is shit, and the world moves on its own after I think I've stopped.

The balls on this guy, right here. Colton Steele. What the hell kind of a name is that? I can't blame my dad for the surname—we had a German name up until the war, Pops told me once. He meant the first one, the one that was supposed to stop the ones that followed it. It wasn't very fashionable to be German then, even with a lot of money.

I can blame my dad for the Colton, though. Listen to that. Colton Steele. Col-ton Steele. I sound like a mustache-twirling villain in a second-rate soap opera. The kind they show in the morning before The Price Is Right because it's not good enough for the afternoon.

This person is a stranger, the one I see when I look down at myself. I'm like someone else wearing my own flesh.

God, I'm going to puke my guts out. My foot slips on something wet. It turns out to be the ocean. That's a hell of a something wet to slip on. I go down hard, rolling onto my side. Combat training kicks in as I go down, and I break fall. It feels like it happens an hour before my slug-gish, boozed-up mind catches up, and I have to lie there with my brain sloshing back and forth in a pool of top-shelf whiskey for a while before I pick up on what happened.

I hear a voice, a piercing call saying my name. It's at once familiar and distant, a soft yet manly voice. That's Julian. He crouches next to me and the setting sun haloes his hair, glowing in the wild frizz of loose strands that float about framing his face until he looks like a stained-glass painting of himself.

Somehow, I'm outside my body, looking at this tableau, this beautiful angelic boy crouching over a reprobate drunk, himself muddied and coated in wet sand and seaweed. Goddamn seaweed tripped me.

Could have been worse. Could have been a jellyfish.

Julian is gorgeous. Beautiful. He's a man and he's beautiful. I let myself really look at him—look at his face. I've been drinking in all the small details of his body, but, somehow, despite all the sex, despite doing things with him I never thought I'd do with anyone, ever, I feel like this is the first time I've really looked at him, and he is beautiful. It's not just his high cheekbones and big eyes and soft lips and, damn, I even like his stubble. My fingers glide over his cheeks, and the scratchiness of them entrances me.

"Did you hit your head or something?"

"Yeah," I blurt, sitting up. "I hit my head and stumbled into a bottle of scotch."

He blinks a few times.

"I got one for you. A man walks into a bar, right? And says 'ow.'"

"Did you just dad-joke me?"

"Yeah," I slur, grinning. I feel all mush-mouthed. "What about the party?"

"I slipped off when I saw you'd gone. I was worried."

"Why?" I say before I can stop myself.

"Why do you think?" he says, annoyed. "You were drinking like you were trying to give yourself a blackout."

"I can't stand fucking weddings."

He sits in the surf next to me. "Why, though? This isn't boredom, Colt, and you're not pissed because you'd rather be somewhere else. You've been rattled as hell all day. What is it?"

Julian puts his hand on my chest and runs his fingers up my neck. When he looks at me, I feel something I've never felt before, ever. Something falls away, like a thin layer of dry skin shedding from my entire body at once. I was only performing before I met him. I pull him to me and at the same time I know I can never tell him something so terrible.

"What?" he says. "Jesus, you're crying."

I choke back a sob. I can't let him…let him see…

Why not? A little voice says, why can't you let him see? Why can't you be honest and open and your real self with him? He deserves it. He's been open to me, mentally and emotionally and physically.

The realization of it hits me all at once in a crushing wave. He gives me his body. I've been inside him. I feel like I've been a passenger inside my own body.

Somehow, during this process of realization, I lean against him and clench my entire body as if I could squeeze the tears back in. At least I'm not blubbering like a kid.

"Couple years ago. Before I decided to leave the Navy. I flew a mission. We weren't flying around fucking dogfighting like in Top Gun. I was hitting ground targets. It was just a job. I never even really saw what we were hitting. The day after one of my missions, I saw on the news. Somebody got footage of it out of the country. I dropped fucking bombs on a fucking wedding, Julian."

The words hang in the air in a near dead silence. Julian has gone rigid, still, quiet.

"Jesus," he whispers. "It wasn't—"

"It was," I say. "It was. I did it. It was me. What am I supposed to say? I was just following orders?"

He sits back and looks at me. "Did you know what it was before it happened?"

I shake my head.

"If you had, would you have done the same thing?"

I shake my head again.

"I'm going to hell. I'm damned," I say. "All day today I was wondering when it would happen, you know? When the scales would balance and the bombs would fall on my sister's wedding."

Julian is quiet. Listening.

It all just flows out of me.

"That's why I never came home—not really. I couldn't stand the old man. It's not his fault. I signed the papers. I was an adult, but he pushed me into it. I'd be tooling around on bikes if he hadn't pushed me. Then I had to be the ace. I had to be the top gun. The badass. The pilot."

"Colt," Julian says, "Listen—"

"Kids!" I scream, my voice echoing out across the water, then softer, "little kids."

"Hey," he says. "Why don't we get inside somewhere? You need to sober up."

"Why are you helping me? Didn't you hear anything I said?"

"Yeah, I did. Now get up."

Somehow, it's almost comical watching him wrap both arms around one of mine and try to pull me to my feet. He succeeds only in gouging tracks in the sand with his heels until I move under my own power, stumbling in a wash of wet sand.

I limp out of the crater I made when I fell and recover some small dignity as I cross the beach to a bench and flop down, then arch forward to thrust my face into my hands.

"Can I ask you something?" he says.

"What?" God, I sound like a blubbery twelve-year-old.

"Are you sure it was you? A hundred percent sure?"

"I've been over and over and over this," I tell him. "I'm sure."

"Tell me how."

I suck in a breath. "It doesn't matter."

"Tell me."

"Alright. There were half a dozen sorties that day. We all hit the same area."

"Could you see the ground?"

"No," I say. "It's not like World War II or whatever. We don't strafe trains and get into dogfights. The actual flying is all skill, but the rest is…it's buttons."

"So somebody that day bombed that wedding, but it might not have been you."

I sit up and rest my chin on my laced fingers.

"When they used to execute somebody, you know, with a firing squad, they'd give one guy a blank."

"I thought they gave one guy the real one and everybody else got a blank," he says.

"I don't know. One of the two. Idea was they wouldn't know who was really responsible. Nobody was guilty."

"Yeah," Julian says.

"That's total bullshit. They pulled the trigger. It doesn't matter if they had the real one or not. They were there. They cooperated. They facilitated. That was me, and I'm never, ever going to get out from under it."

Julian is quiet.

"I don't know what to say," he says. "You were fighting a war. People get hurt. I don't want to talk about it like I know it. Have you talked to anyone else about this? Karen?"

"What would I even say? You know she actually looked up to me once?"

After a silence, I say, "I need a drink."

"No," he says very softly, "You don't."

I scrub my face with my hands, as if trying to grind off the flesh of my cheeks with the callouses on my palms.

"You know what the worst thing is?"

"What?"

"All the praise. The back slaps. The adoring women trying to be cute asking me about flying planes. Do you have any idea what it's like, when the only thing anybody actually seems to like you for is something monstrous?"

"I have no idea what that must feel like," Julian says calmly. "I hope I never find out. I can see it's eating you alive, though."

"Yeah," I say.

Fucking booze makes me all weepy, emotional. Or maybe it's him. I feel like confessing to this man. He just listens.

"I drink all the time. I never really stop. The flight here was the longest I've been without something to drink since I left the military."

"Yeah, I knew you could throw it back," he says. "I wasn't judging. Karen has herculean drinking tolerance, too. I figured it runs in the family."

I snort. "It does. Dad always has a drink in his hand, too. Always expensive. I used to sneak nips of whiskey from his decanters and pour in water. He never noticed."

Julian laughs. "Good. He deserves it."

I lift my head from my hands. The world tilts and sways even though I'm not moving. My throat is dry, trying to cling to itself while I breathe, like twisted up plastic wrap. Everything is numb except what matters.

"I don't think you're a monster," he says.

"Why? Because I'm good in bed?"

He laughs, sadly.

"No. If you were a monster, none of this would bother you. Monsters are just people who do bad things, they're people who do bad things because they want to, they like it. That's not you. You know no matter how fast you kill your liver, it's not going to undo whatever you think you did."

"Something has to happen to me," I say, resigned. "Scales have to balance somehow. Doesn't feel right that I can have all this money and privilege and power and..."

I look at him, at this beautiful angelic man who watches me spill my guts with such compassion, even as I desperately fight the urge to spill my guts more literally all over my shoes. I had too much and it's trying to fight its way back out.

"I have an idea," Julian says. "Instead of waiting for something terrible to happen, why don't you do something proactive to balance the scales. Stop trying to hurt yourself."

"I'm not—"

"Yeah, you are. Tell me you enjoy drinking like this. Go ahead, tell me."

I can't. I only sigh.

"Like what?"

"Start a charity."

"Dad would shit a chicken if I suggested giving away money."

"You can do that eventually, but you have a name and a lot of resources. You could make a real difference in the world. Do you have something better to do?"

I blink a few times.

"No," I say. "Not really. I don't."

"Okay," he says, wrapping his arms around one of mine again. "Let's get you inside before you puke all over the beach."

When I stand up, the swaying is lessened, but still there. I've reached that point in a bender where I need to drink more or I am going to get very sick. Anymore, that point seems to arrive sooner, and the sickness is more intense.

After a few steps, I can walk on my own. The walk back to the hotel feels like a death march. Neither one of us speaks, no agreement is made, but I join Julian in his room, sliding in through the glass doors so no one sees us. I shed my muck-soaked clothes in a pile near the door.

"Hot shower," he says. "Are you okay? You're not going to fall?"

"No. I really need another drink."

"You don't," he says. "I'll get you something. Clean up and lie down on the bed."

The hot water is too much for me. I end up ducking under a cold spray instead, then I turn it up to lukewarm. Just enough to scrub off. I feel cleaner outside but still dirty inside, like my joints have opened up and filled with grit and rocks that crackle and pop when I move. The world's sounds are dulled and my body's protests are loud and creaky. I feel a million years old. I throw back the sheet and lie on his bed on top of a towel.

Something magical happens. An angelic figure lights up the room. Julian, having changed his own sandy clothes, sits on the side of the bed and offers me a glass of red juicy. The sweet tartness of the cranberry sends an involuntary shiver through my body.

"Drink," he says.

"Why?"

"Some of Mom's old wisdom. Cranberry juice. The stuff that makes it red, I don't remember what it's called. Flavonoids or something like that. It'll keep you from getting too bad of a headache.

"I don't think anything can stop that now," I say.

"Yeah."

He makes me down a glass, then another. When I wave off a third, he switches to water.

"Are you trying to make me piss the bed in my sleep?"

"I'm trying to keep you from getting dehydrated. When your liver processes out the alcohol it's going to pull a lot of water out of the rest of your tissues. Part of the headache you feel when you get hung over is dehydration. The pain is your cells shriveling up from lack of water."

"Jesus, you know a lot about this."

"My mom knew how to deal with a drinker," he says, his voice catching just slightly.

I groan, but don't press him.

"I guess if we're unburdening ourselves," he says. "My father died in a car accident. He was drunk."

I suck in a breath. "Was anyone else hurt?"

Julian shakes his head. "One car accident. Wrapped his Plymouth around a tree."

"I'm sorry," I mutter.

"It was worse for my mom and my older siblings. I barely knew him. They'd separated before he died. He left no long after my youngest brother was born."

"I can't imagine what all that must have been like for you," I croak.

"Honestly?" he says. "I don't think the youngest of us really knew anything about it. We didn't know we were poor. Sure, it was falling apart, but we had a big house, and we had a car and Mom saved up to buy one for us to share as we became old enough to drive."

"What happened to it?"

"After we had to sell the house, one of my brothers took it. We sold hers. No one wanted it."

Without prompting, he adds, "It was a Camaro. An '87, but still a Camaro. Mom was a cool mom."

"I can tell you miss her a lot," I say.

"I miss having family. Karen has been the only person in my life for a long time. Things weren't easy between us. Big personalities, and not enough room for everyone. We started splitting off, or making plans to, even before we lost Mom."

"Are you all...?" I start, before I realize how dumb of a question that is."

"Gay?" he says, smirking. "Funny you ask. Yeah, all but one. My sister is straight. I think."

"You think?"

"She's never had a boyfriend. She only cares about this bakery she wants to open. Maybe she's a cupcakeosexual."

I snort.

"I'm going to change and put in an appearance at the reception," he says. "Try to get some rest. Stay away from the honor bar. I mean it."

My only answer is a groan. I'm too tired and too sauced to do much else. Every time my throat feels a little dry, I take more water, but beyond that I don't touch any more drink. After a while I start to fall into a drunk sleep, the fitful light sleep that comes from the fatigue of inebriation but never does that satisfying deep-dive into total, blissful depth.

I awaken with a start. The world turns. My throat is sandpaper, my mouth is Styrofoam, my tongue cardboard. I slug back some water and lay back. I was so intent on slaking that thirst I barely noticed Julian. He lies curled up against my side, warm skin pressed to me, an arm thrown casually over my chest.

How can he want me like that after everything I just told him? How can I possibly be desirable to him? To anyone?

"My head hurts," he mutters, his breath tickling my skin.

"I feel pretty good," I mumble, surprised.

"How good?" he says. "This good?"

His hand skims under the sheet, and, since I'm wearing nothing under it, easily finds his way to my cock. His fingers slip under it and barely does it rest on his palm before my pulse seems to draw from my head and slide down my body to settle between my legs with growing, heavy urgency.

Julian rises on his arm, moving languidly in the morning gloom. Rolling on top of me, he glides between my legs, pushing the sheets down with him. The underside of my shaft slides against his chest. He takes me in both hands and strokes them together, holding the tip inches from his lips in a ball-clenching tease.

"I see my hangover cure works."

I mumble something, but it melts into a moan as his lips wrap around the tip of my dick. When he makes contact, everything is forgotten, and all sensation and energy in my body focuses in a vortex between my legs. His mouth is amazing, warm and hot and slick, lips and tongue moving together masterfully to eke pleasure out of me.

My eyes lock on him, watching my shaft stretch his lips. When he takes me out of his mouth and looks at it, it juts above his hand, ridged with veins and pulsing. Warmth and softness envelopes me, followed by hard suction as he returns to the task. I groan.

He looks up at me with his gorgeous eyes and slips a hand under my body.

For a moment I wonder what he's doing, and then I know. His finger slips up my ass, pressing inside me. He quickly finds a pressure point and it seems to shove pleasure up through my cock into his mouth, but he hasn't come yet.

His head bobs. I watch my cock thrusting between his lips and start to anticipate his motions with little jerks. He pumps his finger in my ass, and the pleasure starts to build, forming a tight, ever expanding knot between my legs. The urge to release verges on pain as it grows—I've never felt it with this intensity before. It builds well past where I should burst, but somehow I hold it back.

I arch forward, head off the bed, then back, raising my hips as he works. Julian makes little sounds, hungrily moaning and slurping as he dives into pleasuring me.

Usually, I have pretty good control. I can last. That's gone. He draws it out of me like an electric shock and I cry out, louder than I want to, out of control as I explode in his mouth. The wet heat expands around me as sweat beads on my skin and Julian swallows, pushing me into his throat as I finish.

Finally, he lifts up, breathing hard as he takes in air. Before he can flop over, I heave forward and yank him towards me, pulling him up to meet my lips. He kisses me back just as hard and writhes, his erection caressing me. I take hold of it and swallow his gasp. It turns into a moan as I lightly stroke, letting the skin slip through my fingers. The feeling of his dick in my hand turns me on more than I ever thought it could.

I just like looking at him. He quivers with excitement as he rolls on his back, his cock lying plump and erect on his stomach. I throw my weight atop his body, pin him down, and savage him with kisses, laughing when he laughs at the tickling of stubble on stubble, of the hair on my chest dragging against his.

He grabs my ass and squeezes as I pump against him, grinding his cock against my body. He groans, spreading his legs and arching his hips up eagerly.

Breaking from the kiss, I slide down, pressing my lips to his chest and stomach and finally the underside of his shaft. He groans hard, his whole body twitching as I give him a taste of his own medicine.

I take him in my mouth as I work a finger into his ass. The little noise he makes as the heat envelopes my finger and fills my mouth drives me wild, bringing me to full erection again.

There is a tension in me still. Slowly, I let it go, and, when it's gone, it's like a thousand-pound weight heaved right off my back. I go from experimentally sucking his cock to lavishing it with my tongue and lips, my free hand, even as I push a second finger inside him. The sounds he makes, halfway between pain and pleasure, make me even harder.

Julian's cock tightens impossibly hard, quivering in my mouth. I slow, watching him. The pleading look in his eyes. The control he surrenders. It's intoxicating, better than anything I've ever felt. He yields to me completely. He's mine to use.

I make him finish and relish it, pressing into him with my fingers as he spills in my mouth.

Even now he arches his hips up, grabs the bottle of lube from the bedside table and the box of condoms with it, and lays them on the bed where I can reach. He doesn't even toss them at me or ask. He just accepts.

I shake with anticipation as the condom rolls down my shaft. The weight of my cock swaying between my legs makes me feel invincible as I work the lube into his body. The expression on his gorgeous face alone is enough to drive me wild before he pulls his legs up and lifts his ass from the bed.

He wants to look me in the eye when I fuck him. I oblige.

I've already prepared him, slicked him. His ass swallows my cock eagerly, taking me to the root as his face contorts in silent pleasure, only broken by a little grunt as my balls press into his ass.

The heat, the wonderful, delectable, all-consuming heat. It's incredible. I rock forward. It's awkward at first. He has to keep his up, and I end up pushing him a little with every thrust, but soon he finds a rhythm with me, loosens up enough that I can pump in to him with his legs wrapped around my waist. He's come to full hardness again and I stroke him in time with his own thrusts, feeling my mounting pleasure building up to an unbearable pressure even as he moans louder and his member gets harder with every movement of my hand.

I fall on him. Our lips lock as our bodies lock, a oneness I've never felt with another person before. I spasm in pleasure, ramming into his accepting body until he explodes between us, crying out his ecstasy as I let loose and finish again, just moments later. As the aftershocks ripple through my body, we collapse together in a sweaty, exhausted heap.

I think I'm falling in love with this man. The absurdity of it only makes it stronger. It's a letting go, a release as powerful as the physical one I just experienced. I pull away from Julian and study him as he lies there, his pale body radiant in the dark. He looks at me with such adoration, like I walked out of a long-forgotten dream and brought it all to reality.

I see him the same. It's like he rose out of some fantasy I'd denied I'd ever had, and burst into reality in my bed, hungry for my lusts and eager to join me in the deepest pleasures I could ever imagine.

"Why are you looking at me like that?" he says.

I don't answer, I just keep doing it.

The sun is beating through the glass doors. Between when we started and finished, the sun came up. Now is the time. I need to get back to my room, and all the better to do it before anyone else is up.

Rising, I pull on my shorts and look at my clothes. Julian rinsed the sand off and hung them to dry. They're still damp but serviceable. It was just sand, after all.

"We'll talk," I say.

"Yeah," he says, sounding more than a little choked up. "Okay."

I lean over and kiss him lightly on the lips. He smiles, but something is bothering him.

"Are you alright?"

"Look at me and tell me you still want to annul the marriage," he says.

I swallow, hard.

That's the thing about dreams. They end. This is reality.

"I don't know," I say.

I guess if this was a romantic movie, the music would swell, he'd make a desperate confession of love, and I'd break down and blurt out just how I'm feeling in a resounding exclamation of my feelings, accept myself for who I truly am, and we'd live happily ever after.

It's not, though. I have to make a choice between him and my life. It doesn't feel like a choice at all, but a nagging voice at the bottom of my brain, crouching somewhere in a lightless cave of a slick mossy rock, whispers: You don't deserve to feel this way.

"We'll talk about it," I offer, lamely, and leave him.

He turns over and looks away from me without a word as I do.

CHAPTER 8

Julian

I don't want to sleep again. I know if I do, it'll feel like I was dreaming. I'll lose the reality of it. I can't stay awake, though. He exhausted me. Colton is the best fuck I've ever had, so attentive and urgent that I start to get hard again just thinking about him. Three in one day would be a new record for me, but I think we could manage.

Once I've catnapped until mid-morning and cleaned up, I go ahead and get dressed. It's parasailing today, or something. I pretty much plan to avoid all the planned activity crap. The newlyweds are probably holding court out on the patio at breakfast. I'm sure by now Karen has gotten used to the attention.

When I head out there, I don't find her, but Alex is milling around. I head over to him, scanning for Colton, who is also missing. Probably asleep. I'll bet that hangover came raging back once the adrenaline faded.

"Hey," I say to him. "Where's Karen?"

He turns from the orange juice dispenser, looking a little shaken.

"Oh, uh," he says. "She wanted to talk to her parents. She's back at their suite."

"Oh," I say. "Oh."

I should stay out of it. She's probably telling them about the baby. Looking at Alex, I wonder if there's any way I could tease out of him whether she's said anything to him. She might be going around plowing the road for a public announcement, making sure it'll go smoothly before she puts her new husband and everyone else on the spot.

I mean, I can't just ask. If I say, Hey, has Karen told you about the baby? I might as well be telling him myself. Even if I'm more oblique about it, same thing. If I just hint about something, it'll set him on edge and I don't want to interfere in their relationship.

"Is something wrong?" he says.

"Just a little groggy," I say quickly. "I had a lot to drink last night."

He laughs. "You must have. You clocked out pretty early. You and Karen's brother both. I don't blame you. Her cousin can be a little much."

"Trevor?"

"I didn't mean Bethany," he says smoothly. "Yeah. You missed the show. He made a total drunken ass out of himself last night. You'd think it was his wedding," Alex says glumly.

"Sorry," I say.

"It doesn't matter. Karen was a little upset, though, with you two slinking off. You might want to talk to her about it. Or avoid her for a while. If you were anyone else, I'd say avoid. She never gives you those trademark tongue lashings. I swear I married a woman with a cat o' nine tails for a tongue."

Ewww, I want to say, but maybe he's hung over and he doesn't get, you know, the implication.

"T.M.I.," I say anyway, playing it off as a joke.

He laughs insincerely and goes to scrape some scrambled eggs from the steamer tray.

If Karen is in her suite or her parents', she'll be on the north side of the hotel grounds. The honeymoon suite she's occupying with her hubby is actually a little cottage. Her parents have one, too, right down the sidewalk from the other.

It's a pleasant walk, down a winding path under palm fronds with a cool sea breeze tempering the air. I wish I knew where Colton was. I need to know what's going through his head.

I wish I hadn't pushed him, but I need to.

I needed to then, anyway. Maybe it was all the endorphins rushing through my system or just the brain fog or what, I don't know. In the light of day, I keep thinking how absurd it is:

Yeah, I think we should have a relationship. I get that vibe from him, too. Expecting that we stay married is absolutely ridiculous. I can't believe they performed the ceremony anyway. We must have been sauced out of our minds.

My reverie is broken by the sounds of shouting. I pick up my pace, faster as I recognize Karen's voice. As I approach the cottage, her voice blasts out through the open windows at past-maximum volume. I can practically hear her vocal cords shredding themselves.

"I thought you'd be happy," she snarls, "I'm giving you everything you wanted."

Her father's voice rolls back at her.

"No woman in this family has ever had to marry before. You should be ashamed of yourself."

Karen laughs, but it's that fractured, strained laugh that's half sob.

"I didn't have to get married. I didn't have to at all. Don't you get that? I could have raised my child myself."

"So you wouldn't just be a slut, you'd flaunt it?"

Her answer is a warbling, wordless yell of fury. I stop in my tracks just as she bursts through the open door, swiping at her eyes. She spins on her heels.

"I should have known better. It's never good enough, is it? No matter what I do, I won't be Colton and that's all you've ever cared about."

Her mother's voice is small as she stands in the doorway.

"That's not true, sweetheart."

"Maybe for you," Karen snaps. "It is for him. My whole damn life, Colton, Colton, Colton. I started a multi-million-dollar company while you weren't looking and I don't even get a pat on the head! Colton farts and you want to put up a statue."

"At least your brother has been careful," her father says, pushing Karen's mom to the side, not too gently.

Karen's head whips around and she follows his gaze. He spotted me, and now she does, too.

"What is he doing here?" her dad says.

"Sorry," I apologize. "I was just looking for Karen."

"Well, you found her," he says.

Before I can make an apology and slink off, he goes on.

"Here's part of your problem. You started hanging around with perverts like this creature. If you weren't so busy whoring and cavorting with sodomites at that expensive college I paid for, you might have made something of yourself."

"Made something of myself?" she shrieks. "I built a business!"

"You sell makeup," her dad says. "You're an up-jumped Mary Kay saleswoman."

"I got an offer to sell my company for twenty million dollars and I turned it down," she bellows back.

"You shouldn't have. This makeup nonsense won't go anywhere."

"I turned it down because it wasn't good enough," she hisses. "The company is worth twice that. What have you ever built? You inherited everything. You sold your own father's motorcycle because Colton knows how to ride it and you don't. You've never done a day of work in your life."

"You would be nothing without me."

"Without your money, yeah. I know where I came from. Mom made you give me money and yeah, I spent it. I never had your support. You don't care about me at all. I'm an afterthought."

"Get out of here," her father snaps. "Try not to rut with any frat boys on your way back to your cottage. Maybe your new husband wants a turn with your little girl-friend here," he says, indicating me with a look.

"That's enough," Colton says.

His voice is almost soft, but lands hard, like a slow but relentless wave. He stalks up behind Karen, shocking me by appearing out of the palms. His legs are sandy up to the hem of his shorts. He must have been out on the beach.

"There you are," their father says. "I was wondering when you'd turn up. I was just telling Karen how she'd get more respect if—"

"Shut up," Colton says.

The old man snaps back, as if he'd been slapped.

"You've run your mouth enough," Colton says firmly. "Karen came to you to share joyous news. You're going to be a grandfather. You're giving her shit for it, over what?

She's twenty-four years old, she runs a huge business, and she's independently wealthy."

"On my dime," his dad snaps back.

"As I'm sure you keep reminding her, since your dimes are the only thing you ever seem to care about. Everything is you, you, you. You have some idiotic idea running through your head about carrying on the family name, so you're spitting on everything you say you want because it isn't exactly how you wanted it down to the meanest detail. That's absurd, and stupid, and so are you."

"What?"

"You heard me," he says. "Listen to yourself. Half the goddamn island just heard you call your daughter a slut on the day after her wedding. What kind of incredible, weeping asshole does something like that?"

"Colton," his mom says, her voice wavering.

"Don't defend him," he says, but gently. "You don't have to just take whatever he dishes out, mom. He doesn't own us."

He stands next to Karen.

"I've put up with the way you've treated her for too long, Dad. I thought it was out of my hands because you weren't hitting her, but you might as well have been. I thought she could take care of herself."

Karen shoots him a withering look.

He puts his hand on her shoulder. "And she can. She was holding her own. I'm not doing this for her. I'm doing it for you. You need to pull your head from your ass, or you're going to lose everything that actually matters."

"I—" he starts.

"Enough," Colton says. "Let's go. You too," he indicates me.

I snap to without thinking. He has that effect on me.

Karen walks away, dazed, down the path. The cottages

are secluded enough that we disappear from one before reaching the other. She swings the door open, walks inside, and plops down at the table in the small kitchenette. Colton sits in front of her, and I pour her a glass of water and make to leave.

"Stay," Colton says before I can reach the door. "Pull up a chair."

Karen stares at the glass of water I set in front of her. Arms folded on the table, she holds her jaw tightly shut, trembling. She holds for a long time, a terribly long time, an agonizing near-eternity of quivering silence before she starts to cry.

"They treat me like this over every little thing," she says, her voice thin and reedy. She doesn't even sound like herself.

"This is my fault," Colton says. "I could have stuck up for you, but I didn't."

"You weren't there," she says.

"I should have been."

Colton motions for me to sit down. I pull up a chair. Colton leans against the counter.

"Have you seen Alex?" Karen says.

"No," Colton answers.

"I have," I say. "He was at breakfast."

"I wanted to take care of this while everyone was busy. I wanted to tell my parents first."

She leans back in her seat, frowning. "This wasn't really planned."

"The pregnancy?"

"Any of it," she sighs, drumming her fingers on the table. "Now I don't even know how I feel. Aren't the cold feet supposed to pass after the wedding is done?"

She studies her wedding band while she wants for an answer.

"Damned if I know," Colton says. "What would I know about getting married?"

He throws me a sly look.

Karen eyes him. "What are you looking at him for?"

My breath catches. Not now, I plead silently.

Colton is either a mind reader or he picks up the same wavelength.

"It's something to get used to," I say. "It's okay to be a little off kilter after…that. You always said your dad was an asshole, but I never expected it to be that bad."

"I gave them everything he said they wanted," she says, sniffing. "Marriage, a grandchild, the whole nine yards. The kid will even have the family name."

"For some reason it's never good enough," Colton says.

"Yeah," she says.

He scrubs at his eyes with the heels of his hands.

"You don't need them anymore. You don't need to suffer his judgment. You're independent."

"You know he's right," she says. "I'm only successful because of his money."

"Yeah, I heard that. I also heard you say it was because of his money, not him. You know you're right. If he'd actually helped you, who knows where you'd be. Look at what you've already done."

"I feel like an entitled, spoiled bitch yelling at daddy because he didn't get me a pony," she sniffs. "I should go back and—"

"No," Colton says. "No, you shouldn't. If anyone is owed an apology, it's you. They're ruining the happiest time of your life."

Karen plunges her head into her hands.

"I just wanted to be good enough."

"You are," I say, touching her shoulder.

Colton pats her head and tilts her up to meet his eyes.

"I'm very proud to be your brother. I know I haven't made that clear enough. I haven't been there for you. I've missed out on a lot and I'm very sorry for that. I'm a lot more fucked up than you know, and I never reached out to you. I'm sorry for that. I want to fix that mistake, if you'll let me. I want to be part of your life."

Karen eyes him.

"Just do me one favor," he says, "don't name the kid Colton, for the love of God. Or Sterling or any other stupid name. Go with Joe or something."

Karen snorts. "Joe Steel sounds like a porn star."

"Maybe something else then," Colton says.

"Karen?" Alex calls, approaching the cottage.

"We should go," Colton says. "Come on, Julian. Let's leave her to share the news with her husband."

I nod and follow him out of the cottage. Alex passes us, looking a little confused, and heads inside.

Once we're a distance away, he says, "We can catch up with her later."

"Yeah," I say. I clear my throat. "I have to tell you something."

"You knew she was pregnant," Colton says softly. "I'm not stupid, Julian. You clearly weren't surprised, and she would tell you first. You're more of a brother to her than I've been."

"I don't know about that," I say.

"Loving my sister when I couldn't is just something else for me to love you for," he says.

"You seem a little different," I say, guardedly.

"I had a long time to think," he says. "Lots of time in the dark."

I nod.

"I'm going to stop drinking," he says. "It's going to be hard. I might need help."

"I'm with you," I say. "Whatever I can do to help."

Colton smiles. "Yeah. I know."

We walk in silence for a time. The path is secluded, winding on itself to make it seem longer than it is. After a while, he glances at me without breaking stride and says,

"Am I a bad person?"

"I already told you what I think about that."

Hiding the devastation of his experience under all that armor must weigh on him, like walking through the world covered in steel plates. I keep my other thought to myself— that until this weekend, he was trying to destroy and punish himself. Now that it comes to it, I find myself wondering how much of his behavior and attitude towards Karen was to punish himself or prove something to himself by making her hate him, too.

"You know, at some point, we need to talk. No joking. Real talk."

"Yeah," he says. "Yeah we do."

"It's absurd to stay married," I say. "Not counting the time I spent crushing on you as a teenager, I've basically known you for three days. If you want to annul the marriage, I'm ready to do that. I don't think I have to persuade you to give us a chance."

"That all sounds good to me," Colton says, looking up at the sky.

Rounding a curve in the path, we almost walk right into Bethany. She stops in place and eyes us both through overwrought fake lashes, her too-pink lips twisting ever so slightly.

"Fancy meeting you two here," she says, sharing some-thing secret with herself.

"Yeah," I say. "How about that."

I bull past her and Colton follows, glancing over his shoulder.

"What was that about?" he asks.

"Damned if I know," I mutter. "Maybe we should have stopped her? Karen and Alex probably need some alone time."

"We have something to do," Colton says. "I want to talk to Trevor. Come with me."

I eye him. "Why?"

"I need to do my duty. Let's find him."

I shrug and walk with him for a time. The air is hot, but the breeze is cool, especially out in the open. The sun is shining, and it makes me feel like I shouldn't be so nervous. That Something-Is-Up sensation crawling around at the base of my spine like a frightened mouse refuses to go away, though. Like I'm staring at a bunch of moving parts but have yet to see the totality of the engine.

"He won't be hard to find," I sigh.

Breakfast is over. Some of the guests are leaving already, catching flights this afternoon. The more idle of Karen's family are staying the week, though, since most of them have nothing better to do. Trevor will be one of those. The way Karen tells it, a fair amount of the family fortune is headed his way.

Colton stands at the edge of the sand, scanning the area with his hand shading his eyes.

"There," I say, pointing.

Trevor has managed to scare up a volleyball game with some bikini-clad opponents. He doesn't appear to be taking the whole thing very seriously. As a matter of fact, he's practically capering, running around in his Hawaiian shirt and board shorts, throwing himself to the ground in an absurd parody of a serious player.

Colton storms across the sand with me in tow.

He folds his arms and waits. Trevor has clearly noticed us, but studiously disregards our presence until his playmates start paying too much attention to the pair of us. He finally trudges over, looking like nothing so much as a kid who's finally been nagged into the house at sunset on a summer day.

"Uh, hi," he says.

"We need to talk," Colton growls.

"About what?"

"Follow me," Colton says, ignoring the question.

Trevor eyes me. I shrug and follow Colton up the beach, off the sand.

He hands me a lemonade and drinks some of his own. Trevor orders a beer and presses the sweating glass to his sweating forehead.

"Hot one," he says.

Colton, with shocking bluntness, says, "Did Alex fuck a stripper?"

Trevor almost falls off his bamboo stool. "What? No. I—what?"

I clear my throat. "Back at the strip club, you, Alex, and Jordan separated from the rest of us to go into the champagne room."

"I really should have asked sooner," Colton says, calmly.

Trevor fidgets. "Yeah, like before the wedding."

"Is that a yes?" Colton says, his eyes narrowing.

"No," Trevor says firmly. "Look, isn't what happens in Vegas supposed to stay in Vegas?"

"I need to know if there's anything I should share with my sister. That's all."

"Alright, we went back there. I guess Jordan wanted to push him into something, I don't know. I just went along with it, you know? I like a good time."

"Point," Colton says. "Get to it."

"Nothing happened with Alex. He left the room. I

guess you guys weren't paying attention. Jordan tried to talk one of the girls into doing something, but she got the bouncer and the guy scared the piss out of us. That's all. It was just embarrassing."

"That's what happened?"

"Hand to God," he says, raising his palm like he's swearing in at a court. "Karen is my cousin, man. You think I'd do something like that? Her husband was pure, I swear. That night, anyway. I don't know the man."

Colton nods. "Good. I better not find out you're lying."

Trevor swallows, turning a little green.

"I'd have to tell Karen," Colton adds. "I'm not threatening you."

"If I find out you're lying, I'll cut you," I say quickly. "Bitch."

Trevor laughs.

I don't.

Colton eyes me.

Then he puts out his hand. "I've been a dick to a lot of people, Trevor. One of them was you. I'm sorry I called you Flavortown."

"What does that even mean?" he says.

Colton and I look at each other.

"Why don't we just move past that," I say.

"Hey," he says. "Why don't you guys come get in on this game? The juggy triplets over there are kicking my ass at volleyball."

I narrow my eyes. "You know I'm gay, right?"

Trevor nods, knowingly. "Exactly, man, exactly. Secret weapon. You're immune to their jiggly charm."

I glance at Colton, and he glances at me.

"Sure," he says, "Come on."

I never really played volleyball. We did it in gym class when I was in high school, but there weren't a lot of beach trips after that. Colton knows how to play, though, and runs me through the basics. I guess knowing how to play beach games comes as part of the Rich Handsome Bachelor Starter Pack.

Some sick amusement comes to me when the three girls Trevor was playing against all eye Colton like a slab of meat, but his eyes slide right off of them. Amusingly, they don't even get the hint when he eyes me while I peel my shirt over my head.

"You're going to burn, dude," Trevor says. "Want some sunblock?"

I look at him, the weird halo of tan lines from his sunglasses remaining eternally perched on his forehead, and laugh.

"Yeah, right, don't worry about me."

"Last warning on the sunblock," Colton says.

"I'm fine," I insist.

"Suit yourself," he says.

The game begins. It's not much of a game. Colton plays seriously, but only briefly, when it begins to put a damper on the fun. After batting the ball around gets boring and everyone has worked up a sweat, Trevor leads us away from the net to the bar. Colton passes on a drink, sticking with lemonade, while I grab a beer with a slice of lime.

A slow-rolling party forms, and everybody is having a good time.

Something weird happens, though. My skin is hot, even when I step into the shade. Colton, already tanned, only darkens in the bright of the day. Resting my hand on my arm, I sniff, wondering why the heat seems to come from under my skin rather than from the sunlight bouncing off of it.

"You look like a lobster," he says.

I use my phone as a mirror. He's right, I'm beet red all over. My shirt stings when I put it back on.

Uh oh.

"Stay in the shade," he says.

I'm so tired. Bone tired; a fatigue that sleep doesn't do anything to diminish. Colton plants an umbrella and I plop down in a folding chair and hide from the sun, sweating unbearably as I seem to bake from the inside out, like a hot dog in a microwave.

"Leave your stuff," Colton says. "Into the water."

"I'd rather not," I say calmly.

"Come on."

"No."

"Come onnnnn," he says, dragging out the word.

"I can't swim."

"It's wading, not swimming. Besides, I'm a Marine. You know what a Marine is, right? I'm not going to let you drown."

"What if there's a riptide?"

"Swim parallel to the shore."

"Jellyfish?"

"Just don't pee on it, that doesn't work."

"Sharks?"

"You see any sharks?"

"Horny dolphins?"

"Not if I get to you first."

I suck in a breath and wince as he grabs my arm. "Come on, let's go. It'll cool you off. You're suffering a burn. Get in the water and reduce the temperature of your skin."

Grunting, I reluctantly wade out into the surf, nervously planting my feet. I'm torn between trying to keep my footing as the waves roll in around my knees and the fear of digging my toes into the sand only for something to crawl out and dart up my leg.

Colton gives me a push. When we're far enough out, I sink into the water and let the buoyancy take me.

"See, that's not so bad," he says.

My teeth are chattering, mincing my words. "If you s-s-s-say so."

He laughs. "Oh, come on, it's not even that cold."

It's stunning how clear the water is. I can see my feet. The few times I'd been in the ocean, only a handful in my life when Mom could afford a rare summer vacation trip to the beach, it was wading into waters off the Delaware coast or Jersey shore, so dark they might as well be ink.

At least I don't have to worry about an eel crawling up my ass.

Colton moves up behind me. I tense, sensing a public display of affection, and pull away.

"We need to talk to your sister," I say, looking around nervously.

He pulls back, waving his arms to open the distance between us in the surf.

"Yeah. You're right. I don't want it getting back to her from anyone but us."

"Do you think she'll be upset?"

"You tell me," I say. "She's your sister."

Colton rolls his eyes. "You know her better than I do. I'm practically a stranger."

"I don't know. She's a little protective of me," I say, shrugging.

"She can be tenacious when she wants to be."

"She must always want to be."

A wave comes rolling in. Colton teaches me to jump from the sand to keep my head above the water and avoid being sucked under. My confidence is a little destroyed when he stands up to his full height—essentially pointing out that the water is actually only as deep as my waist, maybe a little higher.

"Come on," he says, moving further out.

Reluctantly, I follow him. I wouldn't be this bold if I couldn't see the bottom. The water is cool and surprisingly doesn't irritate my skin, despite the salt. Still, I feel the burn on my face. I end up ducking under the water to cool it and come back up with a mop of wet hair.

Colton looks incredible in the water. It plaits his hair to his head and smooths the dark hairs of his chest and stomach to his body, making him sleek like some powerfully elusive and beautiful sea creature. A merman king come up from the depths to drag me off to his kingdom. Keeping my hands off him is hard.

There are other couples in the water. There would be, this is a couples-ey place. They look like they're all starring in their own little romantic resort commercial. Trevor has somehow managed to talk all three volleyball babes out into the water with him and is currently regaling them with tales of…something, as he rises and falls with the waves.

I can't help but wonder where Karen is. This is the first time I feel like this whole thing has actually been fun, people are actually enjoying themselves, and the bride and groom are missing.

Colton looks around. Maybe he noticed, too.

It's getting late. Somehow, the whole day passed. I drag myself out of the water, shocked by how heavy I am once I'm no longer buoyant as I'm forced to crawl.

Colton, as he emerges from the ocean, looks like a model. He runs his fingers through his hair and the puff of water droplets around his head briefly haloes into a tiny rainbow. I just stare, open-mouthed.

"Getting thirsty there, Julian?" Trevor calls.

I stick my tongue out at him.

"Come on," Colton says. "Hopefully we can go talk to Karen."

Shivering, I walk inland with him towards the cottages. I know it's still hot outside, but the air is sucking all the moisture off my skin and it feels like it's in the fifties all of a sudden.

"Might as well change," Colton says, veering towards the rooms.

"Yeah," I say, sensing a subtle undertone to his voice.

Playtime.

I follow him inside. The hotel is deserted.

Except for Karen, seated at a table on the courtyard patio.

She clears her throat.

"We need to talk," she says.

CHAPTER 9

COLTON

Karen, legs crossed, one arm draped over the back of her chair, bears a striking familial resemblance to my father when she stares me down like this. Sometimes, I wonder if that's why we grew apart—I see shades of him in her eyes when she's angry. It's silly, I tell myself, because she is nothing like him. She's a good person and deserves a better brother who isn't slowly poisoning himself and running around the world hiding from his own guilt.

Julian squeaks. Literally. He lets out a little chirping sound.

"About what?" he says, before I can.

"Sit down," she says.

I think, in another life, Karen would have been a deeply feared and respected elementary school teacher. It probably comes in handy, running her own company, to have the kind of voice that makes people snap to attention and follow directions without thinking.

Hell, she should have joined the military, not me. She'd be a general by now.

Calmly, I take a seat. Julian joins me. Karen fingers a can of Coke, and I want to slap myself. She hasn't touched a drink the entire time we were in Las Vegas, nor here, not even at the wedding reception yesterday. She wouldn't, she's too responsible to drink when she's pregnant. Then again, I never knew her to be a lush.

"Somebody tell me what the hell is going on," she says, her voice even but cold.

"We got married," Julian blurts.

"Oh, for fuck's sake," I snap before I can stop myself.

Julian looks at me, and shrugs.

Karen stares at him.

"You're going to look like a lizard tomorrow, you know that? Why aren't you wearing sunblock?"

He opens his mouth but closes it when she keeps speaking.

"This is a joke, right? What the hell do you mean, married?"

"Well," I say. "You see, what happened was…"

I glance at Julian.

"The night of the bachelor party," Julian says calmly, "we got drunk. We hooked up. Things got a little weird. We don't remember very much. We woke up the next morning with a marriage certificate from one of those drive-up chapels."

Karen's mouth falls open.

"Um," I say.

"I can't believe this," she says. "What the hell is wrong with you?"

"Um," Julian says.

"Why didn't you tell me?"

"I didn't want to take away from your big event," I say.

"The last thing either of us would want is to ruin your wedding, Karen. We'd hoped to take care of this quietly and get things taken care of after we leave Florida."

"Taken care of?" I say.

"Annulled," Julian says. "I'm sure it happens all the time. We don't want to cause any potential weirdness."

"How did you find out?" I say.

Karen snorts. "Are you kidding me? Sneaking off together, staring at each other, the way you looked at one another this morning? Jesus, you need to be more careful. You were in the same room as Mom and Dad."

"Our father," I say, "is so far up his own ass that I could have walked into the cottage wearing a rainbow flag cape and started pounding Julian on the table and he would not have noticed."

Karen winces and slaps her hands over her ears.

"Eeuuuugh," she says. "My brother and my best friend. God. I do not want to hear anything about positions or who does what, okay?"

"Why not?" Julian says defensively.

"Do I tell you what orifices Alex sticks it in?"

Julian shudders. "Okay, fine, I take your point."

"I'm not saying there's anything wrong with it, just... my brother and my best friend, you know? I really don't need to know. Just let me say I'm happy for you and take it gracefully."

"You...you are?" Julian says.

"You are?" I repeat.

She looks from one of us to the other.

"I don't hate you, Colton. Thinking about what you said this morning...I don't know what's been eating you all this time, but part of me was mad at you because I knew you were self-destructing. Drunk texting me pictures of yourself with bikini girls in Dubai at three in the morning is a cry for help. Who shares booty calls with his sister?"

Julian turns red. Redder. I glance his way.

"That part of my life is over," I say firmly. "Things have changed."

"Well good, great, I'm glad to hear this. Now what are you going to do about this? When Dad hears about this, he's going to shit a live duck."

"I don't care," I say firmly. "Look...we made an adult decision. It's ludicrous for us to stay married after that fiasco, but we're going to give things a chance. Play it out naturally. Maybe revisit the matter later at its proper time."

We actually didn't discuss that part. Julian snaps his eyes to me.

"Did you just propose?"

"No," I say, blinking. "Besides, I can't propose. We're already married."

"Yes, but we're getting it annulled."

"I know—"

"Enough," Karen says. "I'm serious. What would you do if Dad cut you off? You don't have a job. You haven't worked since you left the Navy."

"I'm a pilot," I say, shrugging. "I can get work. You know the last thing I ever want to be is him."

Karen nods.

"Hell," I say. "Maybe if I put it to him clearly, he'll accept it. Or look the other way. I mean, we could adopt."

"Hey," Julian says, "slow down a little."

I look at him. "It's Sunday. On Friday, you wanted to stay married to me forever."

"That's not fair, your penis does weird things to me."

"I don't want to hear what his penis does to you!" Karen says, her voice high and squeaky. "No penis talk."

"Karen," Julian says blithely, "you've given me enough

details on your boyfriends' dicks for me to draw a composite sketch."

"Gah!" I cry.

"See?" Karen says, "At least you get it!"

"Fine," I say. "No dick talk in front of siblings."

"Fine," Julian sighs. "The one time I'm really happy with a top, I can't even brag."

"Oh God," Karen says, "Oh God, just stop."

Julian grins.

"Okay," he says. "Come on, that was too juicy to let it go. Much like Colton's big thick—"

"Julian!" Karen hisses.

"…hair," he finishes.

"That doesn't even make sense," I say.

"Oh yes, it does," Julian disagrees. "I've been meaning to ask if you use product."

"Product?"

Karen scrubs her face with her hands.

"Can we change the subject? Please?"

"Yes," I say firmly.

"If we must," Julian says slyly.

"Now that everything is out in the open," she says, "I'm pregnant, my brother is gay or…are you bi?"

I shrug.

"Whatever, is there anything else anybody needs to tell anyone else? Anybody? Julian?"

"Nope," he says.

"I want to announce my pregnancy tonight. I don't give a shit if Dad thinks I'm a slut or something, he can go hide in his cottage and jerk off to cigar magazines or whatever he does."

Julian snorts. I chuckle a little.

"Good one," I say. "So, what do you need from us?"

"Nothing, just your bodies."

Julian raises an eyebrow.

"I mean your presence." She checks the tiny watch she always wears on her wrist, "in an hour or so? Out here on the patio. Alex is already telling his people and texting everyone to get together. I'll take care of our family."

"You could just not tell Mom and Dad," I say.

She bites her lip.

"I thought about it," she says. "You never know if he's going to make a scene or not. He just says whatever pops into his head."

"If he doesn't know already, leave him out. If he complains, you can tell him why," I say.

"Yeah," she says. "Yeah, that's a good idea."

"You don't need to worry about him and what he thinks," I say, choking up a little. "You've done extraordinary things. I hope that from now on, I can be a bigger part of your life."

"You should visit us in Seattle after the honeymoon," she says, then she glances at Julian. "Or will you be there already?"

Julian shrugs. "Maybe," he says. "My apartment's a little small. That's okay, though. Colton is pretty adept at fitting himself into tight spaces."

Her eyes narrow. "I told you—"

"You have a dirty mind," Julian says, snapping to his feet. "I'd better go get changed and coat my entire body in lotion."

He drags his fingers over my shoulder as he passes.

"I'll see you later, huh?"

"Yeah," I say.

After he's gone, I start to stand. Karen says, "Don't go."

I sit back down.

"You're not going to hurt him, are you?"

"Never," I say.

"Good, because if you do, I'll stab you. Go. I'll see you in an hour."

Rising, yawning, I head back to my room. There, I scrub down from the seawater and sand and change into light board shorts and a gauzy linen Henley. Despite the heat outside, and the cool hissing rush of air conditioning inside, I want to be out under the sun, free of roofs and walls. I take a seat on the patio outside my door and close my eyes, not intending to drift off to sleep.

Julian shakes me awake. I wince; my shoulder is tender. I'm getting a bit of a burn too, I think. He looks alright, except he's wincing when he moves. Just barely, like he doesn't want to show weakness.

"You're going to have a grand old time with that skin," I say.

"Shut up," he says. "You could have said something."

"As I recall, I did. You should listen to me."

"You should make me," he says, strolling towards the courtyard.

I follow, eagerly, behind him. Somehow, I contain myself, forcing a calm stride, restraining my hands so I don't pinch or slap his ass. I can't put on too much of a show. I'm not sure how open we should be.

The old man should at least have a chance. Hell, it might do Karen a favor. Maybe if he realizes a grandson from his firstborn isn't on the table—a biological one, anyway—he'll get his shit wired tight and apologize to Karen before she cuts him off from the only grandkid he may ever have.

Yeah. We should be the ones cutting him off. Neither one of us needs him anymore. He's hung that over our heads our entire lives, and for what? To seek an approval that will be forever hanging just out of reach like some sadistic punishment in a fable?

A crowd has gathered in the courtyard. Most of the wedding guests have arrived. More trickle in every moment. Karen has taken pride of place at a table with the setting sun behind her and her husband, chatting amiably with another cousin while everyone fills in.

My parents arrive nearly last. My mother hides behind oversized, insectoid sunglasses and a huge floppy hat, holding her purse in front of her belly like a shield. My father is thin-lipped and has a sour expression, like he's ready to unleash a load of whatever onto the nearest convenient target. Probably still upset about the kid.

Karen's right, he'll find an excuse. If I got someone pregnant and then married them after I found out, he'd be jubilant. It's so bitterly unfair that heat flares in my chest, like a burst of embers stoked like a fire. I almost take a step towards him before I restrain myself and take a seat next to Julian.

No, whatever scrapping passes between my father and myself can wait until later. This is Karen's moment, and if the one persnickety asshole in the back has to be sour about it, that's his problem, not everyone else's.

Karen rises wearily and taps a fork to her glass.

"Hey, everybody," she says. "Everyone."

The courtyard goes quiet. Karen bears the attention with practiced ease. She's happier than I've seen her yet, radiant somehow. Everything seems like it's going to be okay.

"I could give a speech, but I guess I should just say it. Alex and I are having a baby!"

A round of applause bursts out. I join, loudly.

Trevor leaps to his feet. "Good news! The boys can swim!"

Karen looks at him like she swallowed a slug. Half the guests are staring at him, the other half are looking away and stifling guffaws.

"Thanks," Alex says, "That really enhanced the moment, Trevor."

Sheepish, Trevor slinks back down to his seat and clears his throat.

"The wedding was great," Karen goes on. "I hope everyone is having a great time. I know we've already lost a few guests, and a few more of you are leaving in the morning. I just wanted to offer my thanks for everyone who came. It means a lot to us to celebrate our love and union in front of everyone."

Alex stands, links hands with his wife, and kisses her.

Bethany leaps to her feet.

"Hey," she says. "Since we're celebrating weddings."

Julian and I lock eyes with each other.

Oh. Shit.

Karen whips around and stares Bethany down.

"Colton," my dad says, his voice cutting the air. "Outside. Now."

"We are outside," Trevor says, confused.

Julian pinches the bridge of his nose and mouths, "fucking Flavortown."

I tense. I glance down at Julian. He looks up at me and shrinks back, as if he's about to dive under the table and hide.

"No," I say. "This is Karen's big day. We can talk later. We're celebrating her future with her husband. Come on everybody, let's have a good time!"

Karen is frozen in place, her face screwed up halfway between despair and wordless, incandescent fury. Alex grips her hand tightly, eyeing the old man with barely contained hatred.

I need to defuse this.

"I don't want to make a scene," Dad says, not taking the goddamn hint.

"Yes, you do!" Karen shrieks.

"Don't lay this at my feet," he says. "Your brother is the one who went out and made a fool of himself in some farcical ceremony marrying another man. If anyone ruined—"

Karen's cry of fury is like a ripping sound, a warbling shriek of anger followed by the sight of my five-foot-four, one-hundred-and-ten-pound sister lunging towards Bethany with her fingers hooked into claws.

Before I can even get to her, Alex and Julian both join in holding her back, and they only succeed in stopping her by lifting her bodily from the floor so her heels kick empty air.

Trevor leaps to his feet.

"Hey man, that's not cool!" he shouts. "Why you have to be like that? Love is love!"

My father stares him down. "Shut your mouth, you fat orange buffoon. If I want an oompa loompa's opinion, I'll go watch Willy Wonka and the Chocolate Factory."

"What the hell did you call me?" Trevor bellows.

"You heard me," Dad snaps.

My mother shrinks back, tears streaming down her cheeks as she silently cries. Behind me, Bethany is cackling like a maniac. Karen is so enraged by the betrayal she might actually disembowel poor Alex with her fingers. The rest of the guests are aghast, frozen in place, and there I am standing there, staring down my father.

You know what, fuck it. If you want it to be this way, it'll be this way.

"ENOUGH!" I roar and grab Julian by the arm. I pull him over, and, right there, I fucking dip him like a dancer and kiss him so hard he lets out a pained "Mmpfh!" from my lips mashing his own into his teeth.

He hangs in my arms, open-mouthed and beet red, as I stand up.

"There, is that good enough for you?"

"This is an embarrassment," my father snarls, "Look at you, making fools of—"

"The only one here making a fool of themselves is you. Jesus Christ, look at what you did to your daughter. Look at her! This is the happiest day of her life and you've reduced her to this. Are you so unhappy that you can't stand to see anyone else enjoy their lives? What the hell is wrong with you?"

"Me? Me?" he barks. "You're throwing your family legacy away for some sick perversion with that boy?"

Shakily, one of the guests, a woman who might be a distant relation of mine or might be with the groom, stands up.

"That's quite enough."

"Who the hell are you?" Dad snaps.

There are other people standing up.

"Somebody get Bethany out of here before my wife gnaws my face off!" Alex shouts.

Trevor steps over to Beth the Betrayer. "You hear 'im. Out."

"I was invited to the party," she says.

Is she out of her mind?

"Yeah, well, I'm uninviting you," Trevor says, planting his meaty fists on his meaty hips. "Respondevouzfuckoff."

She turns on her heels and strides out of the room. I have no idea what she intended to accomplish with that.

Karen finally starts to calm. She looks over at Dad through tear-reddened eyes.

"You need to leave now or I'm calling security."

"You're cut off," he says, "Both of you."

I look at him evenly, my gaze level, my chest proud. Julian stares at me.

"Yeah," I say. "Good. Feeling's mutual."

"You'll regret this," he says. "You need me, boy."

"I know you think that, but nah," I say. "You leaving or what?"

Hotel security finally shows up, milling around at the edge of the patio.

Dad stares me down.

"George," Mom says. "We need to go."

He looks at her like a piece of gum on the bottom of his shoe started talking and turns on his heels, stalking away. Mom hesitates for a moment, starts towards him… and stops, mid-step.

She walks over to Karen's table and throws her arms around my sister.

I walk over and embrace them both.

"I'm so sorry," I say.

"You don't need to be sorry," Karen says. "I guess the party is over."

If it's not, it's the most awkward party in human history. At least half the guests have slunk off, slipping away from all the drama before things escalated. Karen looks around the courtyard.

"I want to go on my honeymoon," she says, turning to Alex. "Why don't we just go now?"

"Well, we'd need a flight."

"I'll leave you to that," I say.

Karen nods. "Yeah. We can talk later."

Turning, I find Julian behind me, watching. I nod, guiding him away from the courtyard. We walk quietly out towards the beach until it's just us in the evening breeze. He leans on the railing and looks out.

"Well," he says, sighing. "That just happened."

I lean next to him and look out at the ocean with him. He rests his head on my shoulder.

"Did he mean what he said? About cutting you off?"

"I don't really care. I'm done living my life for him. It's brought me nothing but misery."

"What should we do now?" Julian asks, standing up.

"Now?" I say. "I don't know. I guess I should think about where I should live. My budget has just been cut. What I want to do, while I'm at it."

Julian nods.

"What do you do, anyway?" I ask him.

"Freelance writer," he says. "I mostly do ad copy for Karen's company, but I have a handful of other clients. It keeps the lights on. I have a studio apartment above a hair salon."

I chew my lip for a while.

"That sounds completely alien to me," I say. "Having so little. But what do I really have?"

He turns to face me. "Me," he says.

"Yeah," I say, "Yeah, I do."

Julian bursts out laughing. "Did you hear what you just said?"

"What?"

"You said 'I do.' You'd better watch that. That phrase has a way of getting you into trouble."

I roll my eyes. "Very funny."

"I just wish I could remember that night," he says. "Was it only a few days ago? It feels like a dream."

"The last three days have been the longest decade of my life."

He laughs again at that.

"I didn't realize being with me made things drag so badly."

I shake my head. "You know that's not what I mean."

"How do you think things are going to be with you and Karen?"

"I think everything is going to be alright," I say. "I really do."

"And they lived happily ever after?" Julian says.

"Not just yet," I say. "We've got a lot to do. Start over, take it a little slower."

"Oh, screw that," he says, leaping into my arms. "The last thing I want right now is for it to be slow."

CHAPTER 10

Julian

"I can't believe this is how you wanted to do this," Karen says.

Since Colt moved to Seattle with us, we've been inseparable, he and I. When he flew ahead of us, what followed was the longest separation I've had from him in six months. In a logistical way, it makes sense for us to have gone back to Las Vegas for this. Seattle in November is charming, but also very, very wet and more than a little cold.

We're not going back to the Keys or anything. I had the idea a while back and when we made things formal, and decided we were going through with this for real, I knew what I had to do.

"Why not?" I say. "We're not the world's most conventional couple. Why have a conventional wedding?"

Karen is hugely pregnant. My nephew is in there getting ready to say hello, not long from now. Alex, ever the proud papa, grunts silently as he's weighed down by all their bags and luggage. I just have my ratty old medic's bag I use to carry my laptop and a garment bag with my tux in it.

"What's in this bag?" Alex says, panting. "Did you bring a boat anchor?"

Karen rolls her eyes.

This time, we skip all the ostentation and obnoxious displays. There's a shuttle at the airport to take us to the hotel. It feels a little absurd to observe the old tradition about seeing each other before the wedding, but part of me sees it as funny.

This should be fun, especially after the way our last family wedding went.

When we arrive at the hotel, the staff are happy to carry the bags up to the rooms, much to Alex's relief. I can't wait to get to sleep. Las Vegas still feels like summer even in winter, but the sun goes down only a little after it does in Seattle, and it was dark when we arrived.

Yawning, I eat a Power Bar from a vending machine and crash out on the bed without even pulling the covers down.

The next morning, Karen bangs on my door five minutes before my alarm goes off. Bleary-eyed from travel and a fitful sleep constantly interrupted by nervous excitement and weird, feverish dreams, I open the door and stare at her.

"Are you getting up, or what?" she says. "It's after ten in the morning. We have to be at the chapel in an hour."

"Yeah, yeah," I yawn. "Let me get ready."

"You want to go down for breakfast first?"

"Thanks, no."

"Suit yourself. I'm starving."

I swing the door shut, shed the remnants of my travel clothes, and lay out my attire for the wedding. After bouncing some ideas back and forth, we decided we'd both wear black tie, but my actual bow tie will be white. A little nod to the notion of a wedding dress.

We rented our tuxes. Colton is on this frugality kick lately. Minimalism, he calls it. If it was up to him, our living room would be one plain white block couch and a TV. I insisted we have actual furniture, but he spent hours drilling into the walls and arranging everything to hide every visible wire.

After I've bathed and dried my hair and dressed, I slip into my rented outfit and adjust my tie. Karen knocks again. When I open the door, she's changed into her own wedding party attire, a peach-colored bridesmaid's dress.

I must have said, "I'm not exactly a bride" about fifty times. We eventually settled it and decided that if I could be her Man of Honor, she could be my Best Woman.

"You ready?" she says. "Are you sure you don't want to eat? They have waffles."

"I'm fine. No waffles. If I eat a waffle, I'll barf it back up in the car."

The rented limo is waiting downstairs at the lobby. Alex joins us on the way down. Everyone else we've invited, a small group, will be meeting us at the chapel.

In the limo, I can barely contain my fidgeting. It's hard not to sweat, even with my jacket across my lap and the air conditioner going full blast. My stomach is fluttering and I can feel my pulse in my chin.

"Why are you so nervous?" Karen asks.

"Why am I?" I say. "I remember when this was you. You weren't exactly queen calm."

She huffs. "Fine, fine. Just try not to look like you're going to an execution. You already live with each other, for God's sakes."

"I know. It' just a big deal. This is a major moment."

"I feel the need," Alex says, "to point out that you already got married once."

"Yeah, but it doesn't count if we don't remember it."

"It definitely counted," Karen says, grinning.

"Fine," I say. "Just drop it. Here we are."

The limo pulls up to a covered portico. The chapel is pink sandstone, surrounded by palm fronds, and, as soon as we step out, a wave of Elvis rolls over us. Speakers mounted on the outside of the building are playing a rolling assortment of the King's greatest hits at all hours of the day. The neighbors must absolutely adore this place.

Karen heads in first.

"He's waiting," she says when she returns. "I'm going back in. Whenever you're ready."

There's no wedding march or anything like that.

I give Karen a few moments to get situated and walk into the chapel.

The wave of raw emotion that slaps me as I pass through the doors almost brings me to one knee. Colton doesn't need a tailored tux to look good. He makes the outfit, rather than the other way around. He watches me with adoration as I walk up the aisle. The chapel is only half full; a handful of guests, mostly local friends of ours from Seattle, along with Trevor's and Colton's mothers. I step up to the altar.

An Elvis impersonator in garb that is somewhere between the Hawaiian Comeback Special and priestly vestments waits to officiate, Bible in hand. He doesn't do an Elvis voice when he speaks. That might be a little too on the nose.

He starts out with, "dearly beloved," and I barely hear the rest. The sound of blood rushing in my ears drowns it out. If I'm not careful, I'm going to faint.

Colton is staring at me. The sounds of the world fade back into view.

Oh shit, Elvis already asked me.

"I do," I say.

It hits me that this is all real, actually happening. Colton takes my hand and slips the gold band around my finger. I do the same, and we hold hands for a moment.

"You may now kiss," Elvis proclaims, and we do.

My heart swells until it feels like my chest will burst. It's still pounding as we step down and walk the length of the small chapel. There's a procession of rental cars all parked outside—instead of a limousine for the newlyweds, Colton rented a Camaro convertible at the airport. The top is already down and waiting.

I ride shotgun and he drives, leading the way across town to the Heart Attack Grill. Trevor made the reservations for us. Our wedding party and guests, together about twenty, have half the restaurant set aside for us. Trevor is practically giddy at the prospect of the food and the waitresses dressed as sexy nurses.

For our wedding feast, Colton and I split the legendary Quadruple Bypass Burger, despite the, uh, questionable name. It takes the two of us half an hour to finish it, and then just barely. The cake is a sheet cake that Trevor bought at a local supermarket and decorated himself...by layering donuts on top of it.

"Are you trying to kill me?" I say, staring at it.

"Nah, it's like a layer cake!" he says, proud of himself for his achievement.

"Wedding cakes don't have candles," Colton says as Trevor lights them.

"Why not? Screw tradition, this is the future," Trevor replies, lifting his lighter high.

"Sir," one of the waitresses interrupts, "Please don't set off the sprinkler system."

"Make a wish," Karen says, grinning slyly.

I look at my husband, my life partner, and he looks at me. I'll ask him what he wished for later. I know what I'm wishing for: More of this will do just fine. We blow out the candles together and Karen rises.

"And now for the toast," she says, hefting a glass of root beer. "To Colton and Julian, my asshole brother and my best friend, who got married behind my back at my own wedding and made a spectacle of themselves while I announced my pregnancy. I don't think anyone could ask for a better asshole brother or a better best friend. I love you both from the bottom of my heart and wish you all the best in the adventure of lifetime partnership. May your days be long and fertile, and may you sire many beautiful children together."

"Uh," I say.

"If you don't, I have it covered," she says, patting her stomach. "The best joy in this world is truly understanding yourself, and better yet is the knowledge that someone understands you truly, in your highs and your lows, your virtues and your sins, your wonders and flaws. May that blessing last you all of your days. Your adventure of life is only just beginning, and together we wish you a happy and long-lasting journey together. Ave, atque vale. Hail, and farewell."

Colton actually swipes a tear from his eye.

"WOO! BADASS SPEECH!" Trevor bellows.

The same exasperated waitress just stares at him.

"What are you doing later?" he asks her.

"Something that doesn't involve you," she says. "Can I get anyone else anything?"

"We'll take the check," Colton says, prompting a round of guffaws. "Let's hit the strip and have some fun."

"Okay," Karen says, grunting as she stands again. "Just do us a favor and don't go get drunk and..."

Colton looks nervously at his mother, who has turned quite pink.

"Yeah," Karen says. "Just remember what happened the last time somebody trusted the two of you alone in Las Vegas."

"Yeah, we will," Colton says. "I'll remember for the rest of my life."

He leans down and whispers in my ear, "I love you, Julian."

"I love you too, Colt."

THANK YOU FOR READING!

Hi there! Thanks for reading my first book, *Mister Brides-maid*. I hope you enjoyed it- it was a blast to write!

I have a sample of my next book for you! It's called *Mister Bridesmaid* and it will be out soon!

If you'd like to sign up for my newsletter to be alerted to my next release, just click here or copy/paste: http://eepurl.com/diXxw5

Ash

My heart is pounding. I wouldn't call myself a bad boy or anything, but I've had my share of scrapes. This is far and away the dumbest thing I've ever done, and maybe the first actual crime. Breaking and entering. It's for a good cause. I'm here to do the right thing. I'll take nothing but photographs.

I check my camera, my most prized possession, for about the tenth time since I peeled back the cheap temporary construction fence and slipped past. I can feel its weight around my neck, but I have to make sure it's still there nonetheless. I take it in my hands, holding it out like a shield.

This building is absolutely beautiful, and it's about to be destroyed. The bones will survive—this building project will strip everything out, down to the iron and timbers, and rebuild it. On the outside, it'll still be the old Reginald Ironworks building. On the inside, it'll be a Silicon Valley workspace. Open concept, lots of curves, pastels, probably a slip 'n slide and a Jamba Juice on the first floor.

This place is a work of art and the thought of it being stripped down to its shell while the beautiful art deco work interiors are destroyed makes me sick. It throbs in my mind like a luscious fruit that splits open to reveal stringy, rotted flesh.

Crouching, I snap a half dozen photos of the lobby. Some of the marble tile floor has already been torn up, but the gorgeous inlaid murals on the wall are still intact. A pair of muscled giants made of all planes and angles with no curves grasps the levers of the world and turns the gears of creation. Bronze tablets set in the wall bear stirring inscriptions trumpeting the power of human ingenuity and creation. It's a living temple of humanism.

All to be destroyed for the crime of not being open concept.

Snapping more photos, I try to choke down my emotions. I'm here for a reason and I'm on borrowed time. The damage I'm seeing is mostly from time—the renovation work hasn't started in full yet, but I can see from the way construction gear and materials have been piled on the floor without concern for the remaining marble that it won't be long until hungry metal teeth eat all the majesty out of this building.

This was going to be a community center, with low income housing, common areas, a community garden, and an artist's plaza on the upper floors with workspaces and studios and an open roof deck for the residents of the neighborhood. Deals were made to preserve and restore the beautiful architecture.

It all collapsed overnight, and I didn't know why until I saw the announcement on the Inquirer website: The building now belongs to Harry Prince and it'll be the head-quarters for his new startup.

My worst fears are confirmed when I peer through the windows of a hastily assembled construction office here in the lobby. It's been cobbled together in some kind of prefab building that was carried in and set up in pieces. Through the window, I manage a few snaps of the architectural drawings, but it's not good enough.

Letting the camera hang, I pick the lock. I'm really rolling the dice here. I get caught with a pick and screwdriver and I'm officially In Possession of Burglary Tools. I've had a few close calls in my urban exploration adventures, but this is the first time I've gone beyond trespassing in an abandoned building.

The lock yields quickly. Nothing sophisticated. My older brother gave me my first lockpicking set at thirteen. He was working construction at the time, so he'd come home with bags full of discarded locks and doorknobs and I'd pick through them. I think he hoped I'd become a locksmith. We all needed a trade to support the family.

I fell in love with photography a few years later. I didn't have a head for the kind of skilled work you need to do to install and re-key locks, but picking them was second nature. The satisfaction of the subtle feeling of tumblers giving way is almost sexual. The door to the construction trailer, unfortunately, is almost too easy. It lives up to the old proverb that locks are just about keeping people honest.

It's too dark inside. Flash photography will look terrible. I swallow and take the risk, flipping on the lights. It sends pale beams across the open floor of the old lobby, cut in crosses by the window frames. When I look out into the light, I half expect the vague shapes in the dark to materialize into a security guard, or maybe the silvered ghosts of

40's salarymen in short sleeves and skinny ties with pocket protectors and horn rimmed glasses, off to win the war with aluminum and steel.

Hurry up, Ash.

Flitting from one board to the next, I snap pictures of the construction diagrams and blueprints. They don't mean much to me. I need something meatier, something to headline my blog. My pulse twitches on both sides of my neck, like caressing fingers ready to squeeze.

On the desk, there's a book. It's full of architectural drawings, very precise and neat. I flip from page to page, snapping photo after photo. I'll edit them later, right now I focus on keeping my shadow out of the frame and squaring them up nicely. It'd be better to scan them.

By my watch, I've been in the trailer for two minutes. Time to go. I snap the lights off and step outside and regret it. My eyes adjust and now the lobby is a flat plane of dark, full of vague shapes etched out by moonlight, like the first strokes of an artist's brush. It costs me precious time to let my eyes adjust. Eight minutes total.

I need to get to the second floor. From the old county records, I know there's some spectacular stuff up there. A frieze runs around the entire second floor. The artist named it the Story of Industry. Just need to find a way up.

The elevators are blocked off. Just as well; I know there's no cars in the shafts and I'm not so crazy as to try climbing up. Instead, I'll have to skinny through more fencing into the stairwell.

Once inside, it's clear why it was sealed off. The concrete stairs are crumbling, with two or three missing, open to a straight drop to the subfloor below. I can't risk losing my night vision, so that darkness will remain a void —no flashlight. Staring at the far edge, I wonder if the concrete could take the impact or if it'd crumble beneath me and drop me into God knows what. It could be just far enough to break my ankles, or a drop down into the bedrock roots of the building onto an impaling forest of wreckage. There's some rebar sticking out of the wall; I don't want to land on any of that if it falls.

"Okay, this has gone on far enough."

Nearly jumping out of my skin, I almost fall and my arms cartwheel on their own. The dark void seems to yawn up at me, reaching out with phantom hands. Instead, a very real one grabs me by the collar and yanks me back like a kitten lifted by the scruff of my neck.

A powerful grip swings me around and then I'm against the wall, two hands grasping bunched up cotton around my neck. Before I can even see him, instinct takes over and I yank myself out of my shirt in a panicked bid for freedom.

It almost works. By almost, I mean not at all. My camera lanyard tangles in my shirt as I try to rip loose, and there is a sudden, heart-freezing lightness around my neck. In the struggle, the breakaway attachment point on the camera snaps loose. The world locks up as I listen for my most valuable possession to hit the ground and break into a million pieces.

Instead, my captor yanks my shirt down to expose my face and holds the camera up in front of my eyes. He caught it.

"You should be more careful with this. It looks expensive. Now move."

I only get a brief look at him in the dark. Taller than I am, he's powerfully muscled, with the kind of athleticism that shows even through immaculately tailored clothes. Very immaculately tailored. He has a key, too, since he just unlocked the fencing around the elevator shaft.

Only when we're in the trailer and he flips on the lights

do I get a good look at him. My stomach drops. He's gorgeous, probably the most handsome man I have ever seen in person. About ten years my senior, his brown hair is lightly streaked with gray and his clean-shaven face is just craggy enough to be intriguing, hypermasculine. He looks like he should throw his shoulders back and plant his foot on the prow of a longboat to lead a Viking raid.

Still holding my camera, he glances at it, and at me.

"How much is Rex paying you?"

Harry

"Who?" he says.

My burglar isn't much of a burglar. As soon as I saw the camera I pegged him for a spy, but not a very good one. A pro would have noticed, and taken care of, the security cameras that recorded a good ten minutes of him wandering around snapping photos of the lobby of my new headquarters. I might have written him off as some punk kid if he'd just looked at the lobby and slipped away, but then he whipped out the lock picks and started photographing confidential company materials.

Complicating things, he's easy on the eyes. Tall and lanky but wiry and strong, his delicate features skirt the line between masculine and feminine and his wild hair, carrying enough static charge to wake up an elephant, is frosted blue and silver at the tips. In the bright lights of the office, the color in his hair brings out his unusual eyes, a light silver edging into blue, and makes me think I've captured some ethereal creature from another plane, a sidhe.

He sits there glumly, his gaze snapping between staring

through me into the middle distance where trespassers and thieves desperately hope to find some way to talk themselves out of trouble and scanning my frame and face in a way that creates a hot stirring in my chest, like a boulder breaking an igneous crust in a dormant volcano. There's a part of me that wants to grab hold of him by that hair and taste those lips.

Christ, Harry. You know you're in a dry spell when your corporate espionage turns you on.

Flipping through his camera yields curious results. He ignored juicier material in this trailer in favor of my architectural drawings, but he also captured all the blueprints and construction diagrams for the renovations. With that material, a spy could slip into the building later and get ahold of something valuable. I've known since I started this that Rex wouldn't just let things go. It's simply not in his nature. He's well named.

A frown curls my lips. If he's a corporate spy, he's not a very good one. A proper intellectual property thief wouldn't use the same camera for espionage work and art photography. He's been in a lot of abandoned buildings. The photos are gorgeous. Curioser and curioser. A thief with a background in the arts. I'm no patron of the humanities, but I know enough to recognize when a photographer has a practiced eye. Half the art of taking good photographs is recognizing when nature and chance hand you a good composition. Kind of a science of recognizing art as it happens to capture and share it.

Oh, and this seals it. No corporate spy has industrial secrets, art photos, and snaps of himself and his friends at the beach on the same camera. I recognize the young man in front of me in a circle of friends under bright sunlight. Shirtless, in board shorts that slip dangerously close to indecency. I'm staring too hard at his shirtless body, and the blood is starting to siphon out of my brain and grow dangerously heavy between my legs.

I set the camera aside and start doing calculus in my head to kill my hardon.

For all the world like a kid who's been sent to the principal's office, he rubs his hands together and stares at his feet. He didn't find any answers printed on my shirt, so he's trying to find them on the floor.

I lean back on my desk.

"Did you call the police?"

"Not yet. I want to know what you're doing here, first."

He senses his chance. I can see it in his eyes.

He swallows.

"I'm an urban explorer. I—"

"I know what an urban explorer is. I don't live in a cave. You sneak into abandoned buildings and photograph them. Well, I should say. You've got quite an eye, judging by your pictures."

He swallows. I watch his throat bob with too much intensity, my imagination running wild with thoughts of feeling the soft skin of his neck against my palm as I turn his chin up. Even musty with construction site dust in his hair, he's alluring.

Wait, does that have asbestos in it?

"Okay then, so you can let me go."

His words hang heavy in empty air between us. I fold my arms over my chest and feel the tick-tick of my arousal picking up again as his eyes skim over my arms and chest, his gaze lingering on my shoulders before he looks away, fixing his attention on the floor between his feet again.

"I'd buy the urban explorer excuse if you didn't have a dozen photos of sensitive information on your camera. This is intellectual property theft. I want to know who you're working for."

His jaw sets, defiant. He chews some thought, grinding his teeth, and his eyes harden. Resolve sets under his skin, turning it to porcelain.

"I don't know who the hell Rex is, but I'm not working for another company. I'm working for my community."

My eyes narrow and I hold my expression neutral. Poker face.

"Go on."

"Before your boss bought this building, it was going to be opened up as a community center. I saw those drawings in that book. This beautiful building is going to be gutted and turned into some slick Silicon Valley work-life balance hellhole full of childish bullshit and glassy-eyed employees that have replaced their souls with company slip n' slides and Taco Tuesdays. Then after you destroy all these frescoes and smash all these friezes and loot the soul of this neighborhood, the corporate drones will come in and tear down the rest of it. Stupid-looking glass and steel townhouses will eat through the old townhouses and blocks and chew up this neighborhood and spit it out. It'll turn into another pit of mediocrity. Guys like the owner of this company don't know anything else but that."

"Oh?" I say, loathe to interrupt.

"Yeah," he says, his voice rising. "They won't stop until everything is the same. No character, no culture. No community gardens, no unique architecture, no history, nothing different or special or full of character. Replace all the heart of this place with manufactured quirky. They're going to turn the whole world into a Starbucks."

"I hate Starbucks," I say, shrugging.

"Then tell your boss. He's probably too busy running a corporate ayahuasca retreat or skiing on his new mountain because his new grocery delivery drones made him a few extra billion."

He almost spits the words, folding his arms up on himself.

"I bet you've never even met the guy," he adds. "He hires you to do a hack job on this work of art so he can spend a few hours here for a ribbon cutting and go back to his private estate, away from plebs like you and me."

I laugh.

"Of course I've met him," I thrust out my hand. "He's me. Harry Prince."

"Oh," he squeaks. "Ashley Baxter."

Ash

"Ashley?" he says, and I groan.

"It's unisex," I snarl, angrily meeting his gaze.

Doing the name thing, again, shatters all my fears and anxieties. Plus, the actual owner of this startup crap is somehow less scary than some random middle management drone or contractor. This is the man himself, standing in the same room with me. His presence should squeeze all the air out through the cracks in the walls and crush my lungs, but he only makes me fiercer. I started my one-man online crusade to save the neighborhood and speak truth to power. Well, here I am, and so is the power.

The power is laughing at me.

"I bet you've had to throw that line out a lot," he says, adding, "Ash. Can I call you Ash?"

He's one of those people who says, 'Can I call you Ash?' but really means 'I'm going to call you Ash'. Pure confidence. I'd admire it, under different circumstances. Hell, I'd find it sexy, under different circumstances.

"You've made a lot of assumptions," he says,

confirming what I was just thinking when he didn't give me time to answer his last question.

"Yeah, I have."

"I don't have a compound. Not a compound kind of guy. I'm not here to destroy anything, either."

"Your type never thinks you are," I snap, my voice sharp with a bitter edge.

"My type? What's that?" he says.

"Master of the universe," I say. "I know all about you. You stand on the shoulders of giants and think you invented all of it. You're so sure that you're right about everything just because your privilege has granted you success that you only ever worry about whether you could, and never stop to think if you should."

He stares at me for a long, pregnant moment.

"Okay, first, did you crib your entire philosophy from Jurassic Park?"

My mouth works silently. "I, uh," I say.

He laughs. "Okay, mister I-know-everything-about-you. Where'd I go to high school?"

"How would I know that?"

"What does my company actually do?"

"I don't know, besides destroy buildings."

"What are my plans for the neighborhood?"

"I didn't get to read anything, I just took pictures of those drawings—"

"How old am I? What's my middle name? What's the name of the company I just left? Where am I from? What's my new company called?"

"Fine, fine," I snap, "I don't know everything about you. I know enough."

"You call me arrogant and presumptuous and privileged," he says, leaning back on his work table, "based on what? That I'm renovating an old building that's going to collapse on itself anyway? That I'm bringing work and money into your neighborhood? God forbid I help someone get a job."

"You won't, you'll just cart in outsiders and replace the people here. I bet you think you'll do us all a favor raising property values, right? Until your neighbors can't afford to pay the tax, sell their houses, and the whole place fills up with McTownhomes."

He stands to his full height and paces in front of me.

"This sounds really, really personal to you, kid."

"I'm not a kid."

"You sound like a spoiled little boy," he says.

"Well I'm not! You don't know anything about me at all."

"You don't know anything about me. So here we are, shouting our misconceptions at each other. Tell me what you're going to do with those photos. That information decides whether you go home or spend the night in jail."

"They go on my blog," I say, flatly.

"Your blog," he says. "Seriously?"

"Yes!"

"Give me the url."

He pulls out his phone and I rattle off the address. He smirks.

"Clever," he mutters. His expression changes as he scrolls through it.

"It's a photography portfolio broken up by uninformed screeds about corporations and politics. You really need to learn to let your work speak for itself. It's more powerful that way."

I stop myself from growling, mostly.

"Exhibition, eh? Have you sold anything?"

"A few," he says. "I've gotten into a few local galleries. I do other work besides my photographs."

"You're an accomplished draftsman. Have you ever considered taking a job with an architectural firm? I could see you getting some work in graphic design, too."

"I do a bit of freelancing. Want my resume?" I offer, dripping with sarcasm.

"Got it. I found your LinkedIn. Nice headshot. You don't look like a punk rock pixie. An actual necktie."

My lips pull back from my teeth.

"You're getting pissed about that? You rant about me burning down your neighborhood and I'm supposed to take it, but you're sensitive about your hair?"

I look away, fuming.

"For the record, I like it. Brings out your eyes."

He snaps his phone back in his pocket and grabs my camera. I wince, my eyes following it in his hands.

"I shouldn't do this," he says. "If I were the ruthless corporate warlord you think I am, I'd have your ass in a jail cell."

I say nothing, until I hear the beep of a photo being deleted.

"Hey!" I shout, leaping for the camera.

He grabs my collar and pins me to the wall easily, one-handed.

"I deleted the photos with sensitive information about my construction plans. I'm letting you go."

"You can't do that!"

"I can't? I've got you cold. I could delete all this, keep the camera, and have you in jail. Tonight. Don't tell me I can't, boy."

I grit my teeth.

"Some photos of my drawings aren't art, kid. I'm going easy on you. Or do you want me to go hard?"

Something inside me stretches out, filling my skin from within. My mouth goes dry as my heart pounds.

"Don't call me kid," I manage, weakly.

"I'll call you what I like. Here's the deal. You go whine on your little blog or whatever about the pretty sculptures and live to fight another day. Just be smarter next time. I watched you from the minute you broke in. Also, I hate to break this to you."

He shoves my camera in my hands and swipes his palm over my chest. Feeling his skin skim over mine, even through cotton, turns the half-stiffy that sprouted when he began manhandling me into a full-on rager, straining in my jeans.

My eyes fall on his palm.

"See that dust? Particalized lead paint and asbestos. Your precious community character is full of lung shredding and brain damaging poison. Terrible me, though, here I am erasing all this important history, not cleaning up an abandoned mess. Invest in a respirator if you're going to trespass and do it somewhere else. Now go, before I change my mind."

My heart is pounding. I glance down.

He's hard. Impressively so. The way he looks at me pins me to the wall, like a deer freezing in the gaze of a hungry wolf. He doesn't make any move to hide it, either. My throat is pulsing with the hammer of my heart and I feel like frigid water has been splashed all over my body. I can barely breathe, and it's not from asbestos.

Well, I hope it isn't, anyway.

"I said go," he says.

Afraid to meet his gaze again, knowing it would anchor me to the floor and lose me my chance to escape, I twist and rush out of the trailer and back through the gap in the chain link onto the sidewalk.

It's late October in Philadelphia and there's a cold snap coming, a quick breath of the arctic cold that will grip the city in a few weeks. In only a thin t-shirt, I shiver, clutching my camera to my chest. I can't tell if the airy feeling in my body, the heat singing in my veins, the funny tingling in my limbs comes from the rush of having escaped something or the sharp, almost delirious instinct that something, instead, has just begun.

THANKS AGAIN!

Let me thank you again for reading my book before you go. If you'd like to be alerted alerted when my next book is released and get sneak peaks of my future releases, you can sign up for my newsletter here:

http://eepurl.com/diXxw5

ABOUT THE AUTHOR

Ivy Oliver is an author of LGBTQ romance, living (currently) outside of Philadelphia, Pennsylvania. In a former life she was a middle school English teacher, and a lifelong romance fan. She discovered the joys of m/m romance after reading another author's work last year, and became smitten with the idea of writing her own.

http://www.ivyoliverbooks.com
    ivyoliverbooks@gmail.com

Copyright © 2018 by Ivy Oliver

All rights reserved.

No part of this book may be reproduced in any form or by any
electronic or mechanical means, including information storage and
retrieval systems, without written permission from the author, except for
the use of brief quotations in a book review.

❀ Created with Vellum

87717192R00111

Made in the USA
San Bernardino, CA
06 September 2018